MW00915263

Kristin's Wilderness

A Braided Trail

GARRETT CONOVER

ILLUSTRATIONS BY
ROD MACIVER & TANYA THOMPSON

Raven Productions, Inc.  Ely, Minnesota

Text © 2006 by Garrett Conover
Illustrations marked RM© 2006 Roderick MacIver,
donated by Heron Dance, www.herondance.org
Illustrations marked TT © 2006 Tanya Thompson
Map and Tracks © 2006 Consie Powell

Published 2006 by Raven Productions, Inc.
PO Box 188, Ely, MN 55731
218-365-3375 www.ravenwords.com

Printed in Minnesota
United States of America
10 9 8 7 6 5 4 3 2 1

Library of Congress Cataloging-in-Publication Data

Conover, Garrett.
    Kristin's wilderness : a braided trail / by Garrett Conover ;
illustrations by Tanya Thompson and Roderick MacIver.
       p. cm.
    ISBN 0-9766264-5-4 (alk. paper)
    1. Minnesota--Fiction. 2. Ontario--Fiction. 3. Wilderness areas
  --Fiction. 4. Wildlife conservation--Fiction. 5. Human-animal
relationships--Fiction.   [1. Wolverines--Fiction.]   I. Title.
    PS3603.O554K75 2006
    813'.6--dc22   2006012525

For Carolena   1989 –

And Janet   1959 – 1997

Acknowledgements

Kristin's Wilderness has benefited hugely from the many readers who gave it their best eye during the long process of honing and fine-tuning. I am especially grateful to all the mothers and daughters for their candor and advice. Thank you also to the secondary ring of readers whom I don't even know, the friends of friends who gave the book a careful look and whose comments shaped the story in many subtle ways.

Johnnie Hyde of Raven Productions found the story through Jeanne Bourquin, one of the readers, and surprised me with a phone call out of the blue, while I was busy experiencing the usual lack of interest and accumulating rejection slips. In addition to being a firm and gentle editor with fabulous production sensibilities, Johnnie led me to watercolor artist Tanya Thompson and to writer

and artist Consie Powell whose help was invaluable, and to a whole new circle of readers who volunteered advice.

Rod MacIver of Heron Dance is heartily thanked for his generosity and interest in this project, as well as his support of grassroots environmental organizations in general.

Thanks also to Bill Nelson for his talented design, and to Bill Jancewicz for his rendering of the Naskapi and Cree symbols.

I also thank Luck and Grace for a bunch of characters who were fast enough to keep ahead of me. This allowed them to be themselves without the meddling I was tempted to try. And thanks to the muses of the various artists who were inspired enough to want to contribute.

Garrett Conover

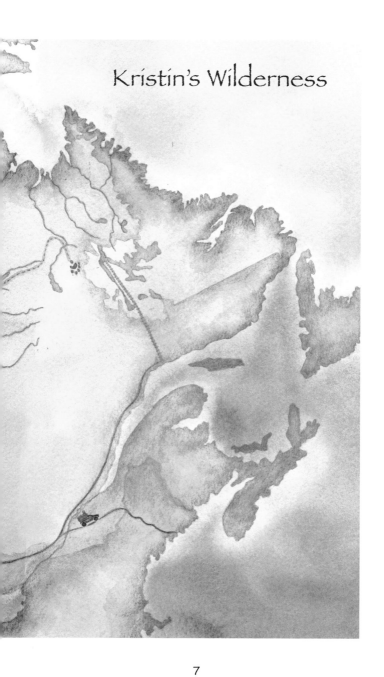

Kristin's Wilderness

Long before any wolverines escaped and printed their tracks all over our lives, Mom told me the story of how some tracks came to be on her leg. They start near her knee, curve up past the big hip bone in front, and end down below her belly in the middle. The only time I see where they end is when we're in the sauna and when we swim. In summer the tracks stay white when her skin gets brown.

"I was your age, Kristin – maybe 9 or 10." It was fall and Mom was dark from a summer of swimming. The tracks were very clear. We were alone in the sauna that time. She always tells better stories when no one else is there.

"My father had taught me to drive his truck," she began. "We were replacing a strand of barbed wire in a fence. Just him and me. The spool was clamped to the bumper of the truck and I would back up just the tiniest bit, inches really, until he signaled the tension was exactly right. Then I'd get out and circle wide to get to him and help him pry the wire to the right height on the post, and he'd tap a clip over the strand with a hammer. I had to stay out of the way in case the wire broke where a kink had been, or where there was an imperfection.

"Once he dropped his hammer while he had pressure on the pry bar and asked me to come hand it to him. I forgot to stay wide and cut straight toward him. The wire snapped. I could hear it zing through the air, and it stung my leg like a whip. The points went through my dungarees all in a line like teeth. They left the row of tracks.

"They used to be really obvious, but when I got older they faded to a row of paired diagonal dots, big and little, big and little. I decided they were some kind of weasel tracks - wolverine tracks. They lead to my own special center. They help me think."

In the soft kerosene light of sauna, Mom talked like that. A lot of the time I didn't know what she was saying, but it was dreamy and close. We'd rub each other's backs or just lie on the benches with our heads close or our feet touching. The lantern hung outside and shone through a little window so that our eyes were always dark, and our bodies and the cedar logs and benches were honey colored. There are always such big ideas in that little room with the stove and rocks so crackling hot.

I call her Mom, but her name is Mari and she came from North Dakota. Now we live in Minnesota where a lot of "our people" live. She says they are Finnish, but there are lots of others too. The oldest ones talk their old language. I hear them in the sauna, the wrinkly old ladies "talking Finn" as they say, and smiling all the time.

Once, in an early winter sauna, I was sitting so I could lean on Mom. That way I could feel her talk through my back, and her arms and legs held me like a nest. Her mouth was close to my ear and she talked low.

"It's funny, how I need the spruce and birch woods, and all the water. North Dakota was all short grass prairie and sky everywhere, even in the river bottoms with cottonwoods leaning over. I sometimes miss the space and the wind. But I need the water and dark forests, and the canoe life and the snowshoe trail. I don't know why. It's like memory. Maybe it's another life I knew and might know again.

"If you follow the waters farther north, the trees get thin and finally stop. The skies are big and the winds can be fierce. Lots of rocks."

"Will we go there, Mari?" I call Mom by her real name in sauna. Maybe because we become like sisters or friends there. And she tells grown-up secrets in case I can understand. That's probably how I got to using big words, too. Mom never tries to make words simpler for me, and sometimes people are surprised at my vocabulary.

11

Mostly I like her breath in my ear and the rise and fall of her belly when she talks. It's like the *Kalevala*, a long endless poem about the Finnish heroes. I don't have a clue what it's all about, but you can just tell it's a big important story.

"Oh, yes. When the time is right, we'll travel there. We can't help ourselves."

"How will we know when the time is right?"

"Because you can always tell. Like now, we have to go out to cool off. We just know. We need to look at the stars and the snow, let the tips of our hair freeze. Then we'll come back in for one more blast of heat before bedtime."

Mom can do things. She's fast and strong. Women like her. Some men are afraid of her, and she likes the ones who aren't, the ones who can keep up.

She's tall with blonde hair - the kind that is gold like sunset on a field of rye. She calls it dusky blonde. It's darker than the bright yellow hair most people have around here, and her skin tans all the way to brown too. She never just burns and peels over and over all summer the way pale blondes do.

I was born near Kalispell, Montana. Mom called it a home birth, and it was in a cabin in the high country. She worked studying mountain goats. I don't remember the cabin or Dad. Now all that shows from that time is my straight brown hair. It's dark and comes from him.

Dad went away with a graduate student. That's when we came to Minnesota. Mom thought she could get work studying wolves, or bears, or bobcats. Instead, she got work doing soil testing. Sometimes for individual people, and sometimes for the Lands and Soils Department. Rich people from Minneapolis and St. Paul were building cabins on the lakes here, and they would call Mom to come dig holes so they'd know where to put buildings and septic fields. She had a little card she gave out and people called her up. Other times she'd get all excited because the work was for anthropologists and other researchers who dig for old stuff the Indians left, or the voyageurs, or settlers.

Once, near a bad pitch of rapids, Mom got to dig in a campsite while a team of divers brought stuff up from the bottom of the pool below the whitewater. I got to help by sifting dirt through screens. We found everything from 250-year-old glass trade beads to stone tools. Part of a broken flint knife and a perfect big point were over 4,000 years old.

At first the divers found funny stuff like a boot, some pop cans, and a Coleman stove. But once they got down in the muck under some boulders, they came up with copper kettles, French trade axes from 1760, and clay pipes in original straw-packed boxes. A voyageur canoe must have dumped there.

At other times Mom got to dig for the Forest Service with a tube-like thing that takes core samples. It brings the dirt up in layers. When pollen and charcoal show up in the older, deeper layers, they tell of the forests and fires that are older than people know. Mom can make the dirt tell stories.

When we first came to northern Minnesota, we didn't have a place to live, but the wildlife research station, where Mom first looked for work, offered us a temporary place to stay. That is how we met Mark and Roberta, and Amanda who was younger than me.

Mark studied wolverines. Not wild ones. Mark's wolverines had been born at a zoo in Alaska, and now they lived in the woods in two giant cages — one for the male and one for the female. They kept them separate because in the wild the animals are solitary except when they mate.

In a fancy frame by Mark's desk was his degree from the University of Idaho. It had a lot of Latin words. While he was getting that degree, Mark studied wild wolverines in an area south of Glacier National Park in the same part of Montana that Mom knew and I don't remember. Mark studied under a guy famous for mountain lions, and Mark and an assistant were supposed to track and observe wolverines.

The trouble was that home ranges – the area where an animal feels at home – are huge for wolverines. So there were only a few widely scattered wolverines in that part of Montana. Trying to find them was hard work, especially in the deep snow during winter.

Radio tracking, where an animal wears a collar that sends out a signal, was just beginning to be used regularly, and Mark did manage to trap a few animals and get collars on them. Then he could use a plane or drive around in a truck and get signals that told him where the animals were. But it was such a big place that even with the radio collars, he hardly ever could find a wolverine. Mark said his assistant always called it a ghost study. "Oh, we chased a lot of tracks around and plotted where the signals moved about, but we sure didn't spend much time actually seeing wolverines." Mark and his assistant learned a lot, but they always had more questions than answers.

The big cages in Minnesota with real habitat gave Mark a way to watch. He and his research assistants would sit in blinds near the cages and write down everything the wolverines did and when they did it — what they ate, where they walked, when they slept, even when they went to the bathroom. They called it behavior studies.

Mark liked to think of his wolverines as coming home to a place they hadn't been in a long time. Eventually, maybe a wild population could be re-introduced.

Mark was in charge of other things too. There were lots of studies going on - some with birds and fish, and others with plants and rocks and lakes. There was a big messy house full of equipment, books, and offices, and some of the people lived there. There were some green trucks, lots of canoes and boats, and even a float plane that could land on water in summer and had skis in winter. They called it a Beaver - a funny name for something that flies.

Mark, Roberta, and Amanda lived in a house that was built by iron miners, and Mom and I moved into three rooms over a garage all full of stuff. We got there by an outside stairway. There was a log sauna down by the lake that was shared with the neighbors along the road.

Roberta worked in town using a big sewing machine at a factory that made winter boots called mukluks. Sometimes she answered the phones, and sometimes she drove a forklift to move boxes around in the shipping room.

Mom was eventually hired to help Mark with all sorts of things. She did everything - driving, using radios, moving trailers to places where people were working. She even knows about boats, chainsaws, and motors. And she still dug holes when the season was right. She knew how to do stuff because of her father and brothers and fixing things in North Dakota. That's how we lived over Mark's and Roberta's garage for free, and what started out as temporary housing became "home".

Amanda became my best friend. We rode the bus to school. When we weren't in school we'd get to help Mark or go with Mom to dig holes. Some of the time Roberta would come too, and she and Mom could talk forever. Sometimes they forgot we were there and we'd hear more than they thought we did.

"Mari, do you know how much Mark likes you?"

"Me? Oh, I guess I do."

"Ever since you showed him how to sharpen the chainsaw the quick way. He can't say enough. He says you grew up with a shovel and tools. That's why you're trim and tough and he likes your sinewy limbs. I wonder if he wishes I was a smaller woman."

"Roberta. You listen. He talks of you with a warmth that would make you weep. He loves you more than his, than his... wolverines."

They laughed at that. They laughed until they had to cry and slap each other on the legs, and then they'd laugh all over again. They laughed so hard it made Amanda and me laugh, and we didn't even know what about.

"You're jealous," Mari said.

"I can't help it. I know you don't mean it, you don't even respond to him. But you drive him crazy."

"He's the best, Roberta. You are the lucky one. I won't show him too much affection because I like him so much. I don't want to ruin that, or complicate anything. We're sweet on each other all right, but I love him like a brother. He's never been anything but a gentleman with me. We talk a lot because of so much driving to the sites when I'm helping. He thinks hard. He's protective of me around some of the men on the field crews, and he's that way with the other single women too. You need to know he has never hinted at anything with me, or any of them."

"I believe you. He tells me what you talk about. He's just so excited. I worry sometimes."

"You don't need to."

"True?"

"Yeah. True, true, true!"

They held hands for a minute across the front seat, to let the truth sink deeper I guess. Amanda and I were quiet a while because we could feel something bigger than we could see in the car just then. So I just sat and wondered why Roberta was always worrying about how big she was. Her shoulders and arms were nice and round, and so was her tummy and the rest of her. I liked her best just that way.

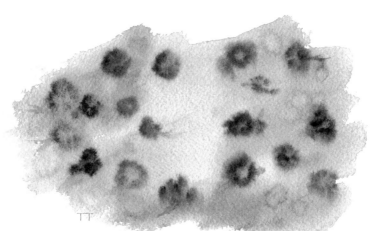

I was trying to learn to paint with watercolors—not kid pictures, but real art. I had found a book full of caribou photos and tried to paint them, but it was hard. So I lay down on the floor of the loft part of the library and just looked at the pictures.

Mom was down below arranging boxes of radio gear for tracking pine martens. When she was finished, she went to a special shelf filled with oversize books. She always went there and looked at books about Labrador and Quebec. She would work really fast and hard to make more time for those books, and at night she'd always have one at home.

Mark came in and he seemed jumpy. "Mari. I need to talk. Robbi [he was the only one who called Roberta that] told me she had a nice chat with you the other day. I didn't know. I hope I never made you nervous or uneasy around here. I can't help that things are bright when you are around."

"You don't make me uneasy, Mark. I feel the same for you."

"You do? I never guessed. I was frightened."

"It's always scary when friendship falls away toward love. You have to learn fast and keep your wits. But it's still a gift, like fireflies in a summer night. It happens to all of us, probably a bunch of times."

Mark touched Mom's arm very lightly and smiled.

"We'll keep each other safe. Watch out for each other."

Mark whistled a bit as he scooped up equipment and shoved a bunch of boxes into a row. While he was doing that, Mom went up to him with an old red book from the Labrador shelf.

"There is something in here, Mark."

"What's that?"

"Cabot's book on Labrador. His companion shot a wolverine in 1904. The wolverine range maps include the area east of Hudson Bay, but you never see much reference to wolverines living there. Even

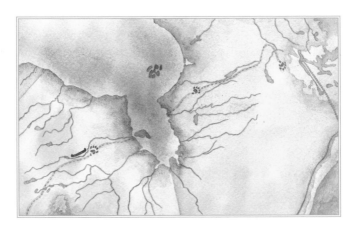

the Hudson's Bay Company records from that area show furs in the tens, not hundreds or thousands like west of the Bay. Do you know why?"

"No. No, I don't."

They pulled out maps and lots of books. They spread stuff out, searching for clues and answers. I fell asleep on the floor, and didn't wake up until Roberta came in wondering where we all were. She said she had a big pot of stew ready for supper. Her clothes smelled of fresh bread.

A new friend, Germaine, and her two boys came over to have dinner and sauna with us. Germaine built wood and canvas canoes, and her boys were like me - no father in their house.

I had always had sauna on Wednesday nights with the old ladies, and with women and girls like Mom and me who came in all sizes. We girls were all skinny with lots of ribs and big knees. But when Germaine came, we all went in together family-style. I didn't know boys were so funny looking. But here we were, and Germaine's boys were as bony as Amanda and me.

After that we started going to sauna on Saturday nights, too. The kids got to sit on the lowest bench where it's cooler, and sometimes higher up if the benches weren't crowded. It was usually a family-style mix of whichever close friends were around. No place was happier than sauna.

"Mom, why do people fall in love?"

"Because love is such a big thing all around us that we can't be near the edge without falling in sooner or later."

"Well what is it like?"

"Do you know what you feel for Amanda, and me, and Mark and Roberta?"

"Yes."

"That's one kind. There is another for places. Like your special tree and special rock, and the places we like to camp."

"Yes."

"There is another kind. Mostly between men and women when they are older."

"That's the kind when you sneak away and kiss?"

"Yes."

"Are you in love with the maps and books you bring home?"

"I'm falling in love with the idea of a place where I've never been, and I want to go there. Yeah, I suppose that's a kind of love."

Mark came over to our house one afternoon looking kind of excited and made an announcement. In a week he was going to fly north into Canada to pick up a researcher who was a special friend. His name was Nels and he had been in the bush with a Canadian biologist studying pine martens. He had been there almost a year and the project was coming to an end. Mom knew of him, but they had never met. Before the pine marten project, he had lived in a wood-heated tent somewhere on Forest Service land over near Grand Marais, on the eastern side of the canoe area. When Mark brought him back, he would stay at the research station until he set up his wall tent somewhere nearby. Together he and Mark would pool the data from the Canadian study and from the work Mark's graduate students had done.

"You already know a bit about him," Mark told Mom. "You've been in his section of books in the library since you came here. Those books about

Quebec and Labrador are all his. He needed a place to keep them out of the weather."

Mom looked very thoughtful and far away. Mark saw that look too.

"You're going to like Nels. He's just like you. A real worker. He stays a bit outside the system, and he does and gets what he wants. He's the best woodsman I know. A little too quiet for some folks, but he's kind. Funny too. You couldn't travel with a better companion. Those maps east of the Bay, the Ungava ones, are his too. The little green lines are canoe trips, the blue ones are winter trips. I know you're not mine to lose, Mari, but I guess I'll lose you to him."

Mark shook his head a little, maybe catching himself saying too much, the way I do whenever I try to hide something from Mom and can't.

Mom stayed thoughtful and quiet. She was thinking something harder and faster than she wanted to. The same way she got when she looked at maps. She called it her crowded daydream problem.

"I may add a friend, Mark, but the old ones won't get lost." She walked over and punched him lightly on the upper arm. It was what she did to her brothers when she really wanted to hug them.

Nels arrived and moved into the swing of life as if he had never been anywhere else. He was good looking with sandy hair and crinkly warm eyes, and not at all afraid of goofing around with words and nonsense. He was always looking at things in surprising ways and singing to himself. At other times he'd go quiet and get a lot done fast. Then all of a sudden he'd be jumping around imitating people or animals or even the airplane, and we'd all be laughing ourselves silly. It was as if we had known him all along.

Germaine came around a lot once Nels was back, and I heard the old ladies in the Wednesday night women's sauna cluck their tongues and wonder what was taking Nels so long to respond. Mom stayed quiet those times.

Mom and Nels were a lot alike. They spent hours and hours together, and could even think for each other after a while. Roberta got impatient with Mom and wondered what the hold up was, but Mom and Nels were just fine inseparable friends. They even went on canoe trips while I stayed with Amanda at her house.

I liked Nels. He was nice to me, and would always teach me how to do whatever was being done. He never acted much like other adults, but that wasn't surprising. Neither my Mom, Nels, or even Mark and Roberta were much like other parents. They just did everything the way it seemed right, and didn't make a big deal of differences or who was who. Mom even let Nels take care of me without the nervousness she showed when someone else was in charge of me. She had taught me to tell her about anything that teachers, other adults, or anyone else did that frightened me or that was odd. With Nels she was trusting, so I trusted him too.

One time I asked him if he could be a dad like Mark was.

"Do you mean a dad to you, Kristin?"

"Yeah ... can't you live here with Mom and me?"

"I can't ever be your dad. But could you let me be a special friend?"

"You're already that. I mean a dad."

He looked at Mom hoping for help.

"Things take time, Honey. You can't just go around appointing people to be in the family."

"But you already love each other. You have for a long time."

Mom and Nels looked at each other, then at me. It was just like the time Amanda and I missed the school bus and thought it was late. We waited and waited. Finally the snowplow man came along and took us to school in the big truck. When we saw that school had started as usual without us, even though we really knew it would have, we looked at each other in that same unbelieving way.

As it turned out, I was right. Not long after

that, the big news one Wednesday sauna was that some of the ladies had seen Mom and Nels holding hands while walking along the lakeshore. Mom grinned and blushed answering to that.

RM

Nels did become more like a dad to me during the next year. He even took me on an overnight canoe trip without Mom, so we could talk about them getting married and how we'd be a new family all of a sudden. After that we talked and talked about all sorts of things. I felt very grown up because he didn't just tell me stuff. He asked about dreams and what I hoped life would be like, and what impressed me and what was hard for me.

But the best thing was when we didn't talk at all. Once on the canoe trip we were sitting on a ledge very late, all talked out, just watching the night on the lake. As it got colder, he took his arm out of one sleeve of his wool jacket and snugged it around us, so I could tug the empty sleeve close under my chin like a scarf. I must have fallen asleep in the warmth and smell of him, because I opened my eyes when he carried me to the tent and said I had to wake up enough to get in my sleeping bag.

We were rustling around getting settled and he showed me how to make a pillow out of my folded shirts.

"Do you have a middle name?" he asked me.

"It's Amber."

"How about if I call you Amber whenever we're on special trips together so we can have a secret?"

"OK, but what will I call you?"

"Nisk."

"Nisk? What's that?"

"It means goose in the language of some friends in Labrador. They are Montagnais, or Innu as they call themselves. I think they called me that because when I was visiting them, I was so eager to learn things that I was always looking around with my neck stretched out. You know how a bunch of geese will be feeding or resting, but there's always one whose neck is up, alert and watching? I think it's that."

"Maybe Mom is smarter and luckier than I thought."

"We're all lucky, Amber. And the best thing is that each of us thinks we are the luckiest of the bunch. I hope that never changes."

When we got home Nels said, "I'll show you something behind the sauna." Nobody did much back there except pee if it was after dark. But a long time ago someone had tried to carve the word "Sisu" on the bottom log.

"We've got to fix this, carve it out so it shows up better."

He had a wooden mallet and a curved woodworker's gouge that was just the right size. After showing me how to tap lightly with the mallet and follow the grain with the bit, he handed the tools to me.

"That's good. Good. You got it. Do you know what "sisu" means?"

"Yeah, those coffee mugs with the Finnish flag on one side say that on the other side. Underneath it says 'tenacity of purpose.'"

"Right. My father would have said 'Grit,' but it's the same thing."

TT

The wedding was at Germaine's canoe shop where there is a big field. Neither Mom or Nels had any living parents to give them away, so I gave them flowers and their special rings. Mom asked me to invite Nels into our family, too, as part of the ceremony to formalize all of us. Everyone was crying and hugging.

For a present everyone contributed money so Nels and Mom could work with Germaine and make their own special canoe. After that, any money left over would go to a big trip they wanted to take after dreaming with the maps all spread out. The trip would be the following summer, and I was supposed to think about whether I wanted to go too, or stay with Amanda. But it was a long way off.

RM

Amanda seemed to get boring and only wanted to hang around watching TV or putting on makeup. I was sad about that and didn't know how to be a best friend anymore. Of course, she was still sort of like a sister because we lived so close, but we didn't play in the trees or on the swimming ledges like we used to.

But then Maggie came into our lives. She didn't wear makeup, or even get rid of the hair on her legs or under her arms. She was slim and angular with long black hair. Really black - so black it had bluish highlights, and was just wavy enough so that it didn't stay put and always looked a bit wind-blown. Much of the time she controlled it in a single thick braid down the middle of her back.

Maggie came from somewhere out East, and played fiddle. In some ways she was like Mom, only more so. Her way was to make life happen and not wait around for things. It was like she was hungry, like things might run out if she didn't grab them. She knew the value of every minute, and made each one worth a lot.

Mark had been awarded a grant to hire an observer in the wolverine work. An ornithologist who was visiting from Vermont to work on a book about ravens had told Mark, "If you have a choice, hire Maggie."

Maggie arrived in a big pickup truck with a beautiful house in back like a pickup truck camper, only wooden and wonderful. It even had a little metal chimney for a tiny wood stove. And there were movable solar panels that charged golf cart batteries to run her CD player and a few lights.

The camper wasn't quite finished on the inside, and Maggie asked if I'd help her fix it up. I didn't know how, but she said she'd show me. We made her a sofa-bed that could become a wider bed when it folded down. She bought a huge piece of foam that she cut to make into a mattress and cushions. Then we sewed slipcovers out of flannel sheets for each part. She bought a long brass piano hinge, plywood, and a bunch of brass screws. "Brass looks better than plain steel screws. It goes with the wood and the hinge."

She was fussy. I had to line all the screw heads up so the slots were in a straight line, and in line with the edge of the hinge and the wood. Even though all that was out of sight most of the time, Maggie wanted it just so. In the end I liked drilling the holes and being careful. If Mom had wanted something like that from me it would have been a bother, but with Maggie it was fun. It made me like her.

With the bed folded up, you could move around to cook or sit on it and read, and anyone as small as Maggie or me could sleep on it. When it folded out, it was a regular size bed, but you couldn't move around the camper.

"How come you need a wider bed?"

"You never know. I might get the hots for somebody and want a place to snuggle. Or maybe you and I could have a camp-out here and talk and giggle."

She was a lot funnier than Mom. I felt special because she didn't make me feel little and annoying. She talked to me like I was another woman.

Mom and Maggie got along like crazy sisters. And Mom seemed to like that I spent a lot of time with Maggie. After school I'd join her in the observation blinds around the edge of the wolverine enclosure. We would take notes on everything we saw. I didn't get it at first. How could we record stuff we didn't know we were looking for? But then things happened. Patterns would emerge, things would show up like secrets and puzzles. In a slow sort of way little bits of excitement would suddenly flash like lightning in a night sky.

As the heat of spring led up to summer and school got out, Maggie and I were inseparable. Maggie got permission to park her truck by the lake just past where Mom and I had our swimming place, and where we would cool off after sauna. We could avoid the road and walk through the woods to get there, and Maggie just walked the shore and trail to the research station every day. One day when we got hot in one of the blinds, I offered to show her the swimming place. It turned out she swam there too, and even kept clean underwear hidden nearby in one of those plastic restaurant buckets. When we arrived she had surprises.

"Kristin, before we jump in I want to tell you some things so you aren't startled."

I looked at her. She was mysterious.

"I only have one breast, and I have some tattoos."

I would have been startled. She was right about that. Even though I had always seen her flat side from the way her shirts fit, I never thought about why that might be.

But I tried to sound casual. "It's OK. Mine are just barely started, and I don't have any tattoos. The only one I've ever seen is on the guy who fixes our car. It's an anchor with the name "Linda" all wrapped up in the prongs."

"Sometimes my scar and the asymmetry scare people." A little quirk twisted the corner of her mouth. "But that's how it is now. That's why I've been reluctant with all the sauna invitations out here."

"But you could sit between me and Mom."

"Ah, you're so sweet. That's just what Mari said. It's a deal then."

When her shirt was off the scar was not easy to see. A beautiful vine with pale purpley-blue flowers and triplets of fine green leaves and little tendrils coiled around it. Purple Clematis she said. She let my fingertips trace the slight bumpiness where the sutures had closed the incision across her ribs.

"It's beautiful Maggie, like a shy eyelid closed over your heart."

"Oh, you are Mari's daughter. You talk like she does, don't you?"

"Did it hurt?"

"The surgery or the tattooing?"

"Tattooing. How is it so fine and detailed and full of colors?"

"Depends on the spot. Some parts really hurt. Some didn't. Some places it was more like an itch, and later it burned a little." Maggie glanced down. "The artist who did it used different needle bars. Those are things that hold the needles that push the different colors into the skin. You can control the fineness of line and shading by the size of the needles, and how many are clustered on the bar. It's quite a process."

"Wow."

Maggie was still swimming when I climbed up on the ledge to dry in the sun. She was quite a ways out when she headed for shore with long clean strokes. Her stroke changed and she submerged and swam a long way underwater. Really long. I was worried she might have vanished. But then her head broke the surface so close she could just stand up and wade in.

Watching her rise from the water made me just know there was something about her. The water had parted her hair, and her cheekbones were angular and beautiful. Although she was missing part of her body, she seemed utterly complete. As if she had been born that moment of lake and swamp and woods. As she stooped to scoop a drink from the lake, the water fell from her shoulders and hips and ran down her muscular legs. She seemed to me beautifully wild – totally at home in the world.

That is when I saw the other tattoo. It was a Spring Peeper perched on the outer curve of her remaining breast. The little round pads of the front foot reached just into the dark skin around the nipple, and Maggie let me lean in close to see it better. It was just as beautiful as the vine across from it, and so finely drawn and shaded it might have been real. Maggie was just like the paintings in Mom's book on Faeries. Her black hair made her stand out in this land of blondes, and I secretly hoped she might be some kind of sorceress or nymph like the paintings in the book.

"Mom, how come Maggie has only one breast?"

"She had cancer. Sometimes, if a tumor is found, that's what has to be done. If it's done in time you can live. Maybe a short time, maybe a long time. If you ask I bet she'll tell you all about it."

Maggie did tell. She said that fear and hope are her companions, not just some of the time but always. "The trick is to learn from everything rather than get gloomy. You have to accommodate all the pieces of life." She seemed so much like Mom and kissed the top of my head, so I could feel her calm lips in the part of my hair. There was just so much to know about, and it was always just out of reach, like the best apples in the fall.

I daydreamed about tattoos constantly after that first swim. Although I never mentioned those thoughts out loud, Mom had that annoying ability to read my mind, sometimes even before I could read it myself.

"You have to think hard about permanent markings, Kristin. You won't always foresee a change of mind later in life."

I must have looked surprised by her accuracy, because her quick grin all but said: "Gotcha, didn't I?"

She spent a long time explaining that to erase a tattoo required burning layers of skin away with a laser, letting it heal, and then doing more layers. It was costly, painful, took a long time, and for all that never worked as well as anyone hoped. And I did think hard about it, but never changed my mind.

RM

Nels and Mom dried food for their big trip with their newly built canoe, and worked like crazy to get everything ready to go. With Maggie capturing my attention, I didn't want to go with them, so I stayed behind. It worked well for me, and I think Mom and Nels were secretly relieved. Maggie lived in our building once they were underway, and it was great fun. She slowly expected more and more from me and we became a team. I ended up learning to cook, and to help keep our place neat and orderly without even complaining too much.

Mom and Nels departed just out of town, on Moose Lake, and from there cut across the Minnesota-Ontario border lakes, north through Quetico, then diagonally northeast across Ontario.

Eventually they entered the Attawapiskat River and followed it to James Bay. Germaine had made the same trip years ago, and they had her maps and notes. It took a long time to go that far.

Maggie and I canoed with Mom and Nels as far as the middle of Basswood Lake where the Boundary Waters Canoe Area Wilderness of Minnesota ends and the Quetico Park of Ontario starts. It was fun seeing them off and camping for a few days. They looked tiny when they headed on and Maggie and I turned back to our campsite. We had left camp set up, so we started supper right away.

"Do you dream of a big trip, Kristin?"

"Not really. I've never thought of it that much. But Mom thinks big all the time."

"I've never been out for more than a week. Just think how far they're going. There won't be campsites like here, or marked trails, or rules. I wish we could be with them the whole way."

I looked out over our fire at the huge horizon of the lake. It was empty. Our island campsite felt very small, and I could feel a big tug in my chest. Maggie moved over a bit and her arm came up around my shoulders. I was glad of that. Then we got busy with supper and talking and joking around.

For the rest of that summer while Nels and Mom were away, I began to feel grown up. Just being around Maggie and the other researchers made me want to be involved with their projects.

I was never told to, but I kind of worked into whatever was being done. The more I contributed, the more everyone seemed to expect, and the more I was included and given responsibility.

Maggie and I built an addition to the wolverine enclosures. The two big cages almost touched in one place. Our job was to make a short connector section out of the same heavy mesh wire, and a panel that could close the connection off.

Maggie said that although breeding captive animals was not always a sure thing, Mark wanted to see what would happen naturally, and only resort to artificial means if that failed. We'd know in the coming April how that plan would unfold. If it was successful and the female had kits, we could close the male off in his own enclosure. In mustelids — the Latin word for the weasel family - the males don't contribute to raising offspring, and in the confinement of the enclosure could possibly even endanger them.

We didn't just make a tube from one enclosure to the next, we kept it irregular and included a bunch of trees and brush, and even a big boulder perched on a granite outcrop. The boulder was a glacial erratic, which meant it was a type of rock that wasn't local, so it had been carried there in the glacier ice.

When we were done and the connection was opened, we spent extra time in the blinds so we could see how the wolverines interacted. At first they mostly ignored each other and spent a lot of time poking around the space that was new to them. But after a few days, they would occasionally sniff each other. By the end of the first week, they started playing what looked like a game of tag, or maybe follow-the-leader.

I helped out with some of the other research projects too. Some volunteer students working with the amphibian researchers taught me to drive a standard shift in an old truck whenever we got off on small dirt roads. We roamed the wetlands to the various study sites for estimating frog and toad populations by listening to their songs.

There was a real science nerd studying lichens. Although the lichens were interesting, and he was looking for heavy metal pollution and acid rain effects in them, he was unbelievably dull. I asked Maggie if he was really that boring and she just about got sick laughing so hard. "He sure is! They call him 'Creeping Death' over at the college where his office is."

When Mom and Nels finally got back, we had days and days of stories. As soon as their slides were finished at the photo shop, we had a potluck with a lot of friends who wanted to see the pictures of their trip. I was impressed with their excitement about getting good at running heavy whitewater and lining the canoes when the rapids were too complex and rough to run. The pictures were amazing, showing wide rivers with gravel bars as big as the beaches on Lake Superior, hills that seemed to go on forever, waterfalls with cliffs all around that seemed impossible to travel around, and finally the flat expanse of lowlands at the edge of Hudson Bay.

Mom and Nels seemed to be excited with how I had changed too, even though I didn't really see it myself. "See," Nels said to Mom once. "That kid is full of Sisu. I knew it. I told you so."

Mom told me that although my summer work wasn't a paid job, it would look really good when I wrote it up in a resume for job or school applications. "You'll stand right out from all the TV and video game junkies out there."

Even the teachers at school thought I'd made a big jump that summer, so I finally believed it myself.

Mom and Maggie arranged an event the very day it became clear that I was leaving girlhood behind. Mom had prepared me with instructions and a little booklet over a year before anything happened just in case, and now all this time later everything seemed sudden. It didn't feel like much of an accomplishment to me since I didn't really do anything, but Mom was all warm and acting as if she were proud.

Maggie and she bustled about all morning, and were still at it when I got home from school. Mom, who never loses her cool, nearly went into a tizzy when we discovered that I had outgrown my only dress. At first she thought we'd never find one in town. She was halfway to the phone to call someone with a daughter my size when she spun around.

"Nope, we'll try one of the la-de-da artsy shops. They'll have something."

She had her feisty grin on, which meant nothing was going to get in her way, and she even drove kind of fast for her. And we had luck. Not only was there a festive cluster of bright dresses behind a sculpture and jewelry counter, but they were all on sale now that summer was over. It wasn't hard to choose. I saw a slim blacky-blue one with lots of bright orchids in splashes of light blue, lavender,

hints of yellow, and something luminous that wasn't quite white. It fit so perfectly that Mom got over-enthusiastic and embarrassing. Then she even bought herself a new dress.

On the way home something happened. I don't know what. I was all excited about my dress, but suddenly didn't want to wear it. Mom kept looking at me, reading my mind again, and it really made me mad.

"Who would have thought it? Even your skin-flinty

Mom got a dress. A sale right here for stuff we'd usually have to get in Duluth or the Twin Cities."

I just looked out the window.

Back home in the kitchen there was thick quiet, like the air before rain. I didn't want to hear whatever cheery little thing Mom was about to say, but she didn't say anything. She made tea and looked subdued, and I went to my room. After a while I tried my dress on again. It really did look nice, but I was afraid.

My hips were beginning to flare, and still not much was happening up top. I was annoyed with Amanda, a year younger, and always arching her back to make people notice things. Why couldn't everything just magically appear so you wouldn't have to hide or show off or feel stupid? For a while I had even avoided the sauna, and that was hard. Nothing feels as good as sauna.

There was a soft knock on my door, and before Mom could ask if she could come in, I opened it. She had her new dress on.

"You know, if you don't want to dress up today, you don't have to. I was just hoping it would be fun."

I didn't know what to say, so I stayed quiet.

"Wanna see something funny? I was wiggling my butt in the mirror. It's hilarious. If I didn't have long legs, my butt would be way too wide for me."

She grabbed my hand and I trailed after her. A mirror was leaning on the counter at an angle, so we could see when we went by. Mom waggled by with great exaggeration and I did get to laughing. Worse yet, I waggled by too, and we got to waggling around and laughing so hard we didn't hear Maggie come up the steps.

"What are you two cracking up about?" she called. Then she poked her head in the door. "Oh geeze! Give me a break. I'm not even gonna try that. All the twitching in the world wouldn't help my little-boy bottom."

But that didn't stop her, and pretty soon we couldn't tell who was cackling and waggling the hardest. In the end I forgot to be such a jerk about everything.

There was a potluck supper with only women, and we fired up the sauna. Friends who hadn't worn a skirt since Mom's wedding were wearing loose summer dresses printed with blossoms and colors, and we all put some of the last fall flowers in our hair. Nels and Mark dashed over to the sauna once with a bag, and then retreated to Mark's house where the fathers and boys were eating their own supper.

At dusk, when we went to the sauna, Maggie led the way with her fiddle. She did some complicated French Canadian jigging steps as we all pranced down behind her as best we could. In the changing room were some presents, including a big fat book of life by, for, and about women. That was from Mom and Nels, and everyone there signed it. There was a set of 36 watercolors in tubes, and a block of fancy French watercolor paper from Maggie, and a letter from Mom to me on a hand-painted card.

We all sat quiet in the dry heat for a while. I noticed that everyone there was a close friend, and only one of the old Finn ladies had come. Maija-Riitta was there to get an extra sauna that week since it was not the standard Saturday night or the ladies' Wednesday night. She was stern and big and never judged much, only observed things. "Our mothers never did anything like this. We didn't either." Someone asked if it was too much fuss, but Maija-Riitta just settled into the heat and didn't answer. Her hearing aids were out in the changing room.

After ten minutes or so Mom cast a ladle of water on the rocks. The first steam was the euphoria-inducing rush of heat the Finns call "löyly." Mom said, "For the girl stepping aside and the woman emerging." The next was from Maggie "for the dreams to stay and grow and lead." When the third ladle was cast without comment, Maija-Riitta said something in Finnish, and I recognized the word Sisu.

Then it was just usual sauna time. Lots of laughter and stories and fun, with a few cooling sessions between heatings. I wasn't the only one that night with a little white string hanging down.

When we were back in our clothes, Maggie led us along the path to the house by playing a beautiful waltz called "Gentle Maiden" so that we walked slowly and the dresses swayed in the night air. The boys and men were waiting by the picnic table when we arrived. Mark and Nels each swung me once around in waltz position. Then Maggie picked up the tempo. She taught us a dance in which we changed partners until we had each danced with everyone else. That was really fun. Maggie called it a "contra" dance and said there were some really hard ones, but since she usually played the music, she didn't know how to teach them to us. Then it was time for ice cream while the crickets sang in the dark and autumn eased toward the time when all the leaves would be down. Not many warm days left.

Just before sleep, I felt funny and began to cry. I didn't think I made much noise, but Nels and Mom appeared and sat with me. When they asked, I couldn't say why I felt like crying. It was just that I didn't want to have to grow up. Somehow they knew that. They each massaged my feet and lower legs from where they sat on my bed. Calmness coiled up through me and without ever knowing when, I slid into a beautiful deep sleep.

After that, things really were different. For the first time I spent each sauna on the top bench in the hottest heat. Maija-Riitta noticed and said, "That's good. Strong girl."

The final cooling was always in the lake, and was even more delicious as the waters cooled in fall. At first it was a silky relief after the final session's heat, but then in a minute or two it became that breath-shortening cold around my ribs and sternum, and through my shins if I stayed in the water longer. No matter how many times I felt that splendid contrast, it was always magical and not explainable to others who hadn't experienced it.

For a while I didn't visit the blinds after school. Mostly I looked in the big women's book. It had more answers than most people could know the questions to. And when I snooped around the answers, I'd have even more questions. It was like a big exciting puzzle. It even told all about women with a missing breast, and there was a picture where Maggie might have gotten the idea for her tattoo.

It wasn't all wonderful either. Just as it didn't shy away from the glorious parts of love and life, it was explicit about things like disease, alcohol, drugs, violence, rage, meanness, and fear. I didn't know much about the good stuff, but suspected some of it. The bad stuff terrified me. I had nightmares. I woke up unable to move or run, and with my heart racing. But Mom or Nels would come hold me and let me ask questions, or remind me that a little bit of sensible fear might keep me alert enough to stay out of trouble in the first place. They always brought calm and balance.

"I have a plan, Maggie."

"A big one?"

"Yeah. I'm going to paint a book. All watercolors. It's going to be all about life at sauna."

"What a beautiful thing. You're amazing, Kristin."

"I'm going to call it A Tribe Like Us."

"No kidding!"

"But how can I paint stories and happiness and sweetness?"

"Well, let's see. That stuff radiates when we are there, and we all know and feel it. Must be you have to show it in how people sit and look and smile. How old Maija-Riitta coils and loops her silver braids on top of her head, and how her whole body sags and folds into smiling wrinkles. Maybe you should just go there and sketch the stove, and the wooden buckets, and the carved door latch, or the joints in the logs. Slowly you'll fill in with the rest, lead up to it. It'll all work itself out. Just start."

RM

The following April, right on schedule, the wolverines had kits. We had known something was up when the adult female didn't appear for several days. Then one day, in a patch of sun, we saw two kits all squirmy and fluffy and small, nursing and sprawling around their mother. We coaxed the male into the other enclosure with a road-killed grouse, then closed the connecting section.

Mom named the dark kit, a female, Kwewadzsho, which means wolverine in Naskapi, the language of some Indians in Labrador. She saw the word in an anthropology book of Nels, and even learned to write it in Cree syllabics like this:

ᑯᐃ"ᑯ"ᐊᒋᔪ°

I named the other one Ghost. It looked unusually light because of strange whitish tips on most of its fur.

As summer progressed and the kits were growing like crazy, it became difficult to watch all the activity and interactivity. Maggie had to work hard to keep her notes, and we got to whisper to each other less in the blinds. Sometimes we couldn't talk at all.

Adding those two kits was like magic. Suddenly there was a wolverine family. We had never thought kits would make things twenty times more interesting and fun, but they did. We couldn't watch and wonder enough. Even Mark was swept up by it all.

"I hope nobody overhears us carrying on. You'd think we had all had kids ourselves, not just watched a big weasel having smaller weasels."

The longer we watched, the more attached we became to the kits. It was hard because we couldn't cuddle them or show the affection we felt. The rules were to watch, but not influence. To observe, but not manipulate the situation or any behavior.

Still, we came to love them. Ghost was visible and direct. If he wanted to cross an opening, he did. With his white-tipped fur he couldn't sneak well anyway, and didn't seem to want to. All his motions said: "Here I am. Watch out. Coming through."

Kwewadzsho was more like me. Not sneaky exactly, but cautious. Present, but not overly visible. Always watching, looking underneath and behind everything. Mom once said I was like a spotted fawn in dappled light – so hard to see I was always spooking her when she'd suddenly become aware of me at close range. Kwewadzsho was far better at that than I was. Maggie said she'd never seen anything in plain sight remain so invisible.

There was a brook running through the enclosure that dried up in summer, and while Ghost would barge up or down the middle of it, Kwewadzsho would flow like shade along its edges in the cover of rocks and undergrowth. If she crossed bare ground or the brook, she would use the shadow of a tree, the slightest irregularity or broken outline as partial cover. If nothing were available, just a speck on an open surface would distract our eyes from the bigger shape crossing there. Stillness, fluidity, and grace were perfected to a fine and eerie art form. Disappearance was easy for Kwewadzsho, and through the act of practicing invisibility, she stole my heart completely.

Later in the summer Mark put an experimental radio collar on Kwewadzsho. It was a small compact one like the marten collars, but it had an expandable part. Mark wanted to develop one that could grow with an animal. It needed to be tight enough to stay on, but not so tight it could hurt or choke. He used a real transmitter too, to see if the weight was bothersome. It came all bright and yellow, but Mark painted it blotchy and dark. He didn't like the intrusion of the telemetry equipment on the lives of animals in his studies, but it was necessary. The least he could do was match the color of the fur.

Maggie didn't like the collars either. One day she wondered what would happen if the kits got away. Would the offspring of wolverines that were never wild have some encoded knowledge of how to live and be in the world?

"Well, couldn't you make the enclosure leak, Maggie?"

"Kristin!" She gave me a harsh look. "That would not be good. You can't do that. They are not our animals, and it would be illegal. It would hurt Mark's work. It would ruin everything."

"It was just a question."

She softened. "I know. And it's a good one. I bet every one of us here has asked ourselves that a thousand times." Her stern expression returned. "But don't get any ideas. You have to make a promise. This is serious. You have to be responsible."

"Yeah, I promise. It's just that I thought it."

August got hot and dry. There were lightning fires in the Boundary Waters, but they weren't allowed to burn naturally like they sometimes did. The fire danger was too high. The Beaver dumped loads of water on them as soon as they were spotted. Outside the wilderness area there were some fires started by careless campers. One of them came close to town, and men with bulldozers made fire lines around some of the buildings on the outskirts. Then it rained, and the fires went out by themselves. We never had to worry about the compound at the research station.

After all that hot weather, a windy cold front came in. It blew like crazy. We could feel the buildings shudder. Just before dawn we heard a crash because a big fir with a rotten center blew over. We could hear Maggie pounding up the steps to wake us all. She was out of breath and excited.

"Come quickly! There's a big hole in the wolverine enclosure and a section of fence is down. Some of the wolverines might have escaped."

We ran out and took a quick tally. Both Kwewadzsho and Ghost were gone. The female, who had never known freedom, was still in one of her resting spots in a maze of big boulders. The male's enclosure wasn't damaged, and he was running back and forth along the trunk of a newly fallen tree. We ran to the house and raised Mark and Roberta out of bed. Everyone available helped repair the fence right away, rolling out the wire mesh and stitching everything back together with wire and pliers.

Then we all had coffee and breakfast in the kitchen. Mark looked excited. "You know," he said, "this could be very interesting." Maggie looked at me, and me at her. There seemed to be a wild light in our eyes. Wind still thrashed in the trees.

Mark sent two vehicles with telemetry receivers out on the local roads, and dispatched news of the escape to all the regional offices, field camps, and even some distant places. After two days with no reports, he was really curious. No one had expected the kits to go far.

There was not enough money in the research budget for an unscheduled flight, but on the fourth day Mark got permission to fly if he did it on his own time and paid for flight time. The headphones stayed quiet on the frequency of Kwewadzsho's collar. Mark stopped being puzzled and became annoyed. From the air he should have picked up something.

The summer work continued. All the research crews carried on, but with an eye and ear out for any sign of Kwewadzsho or Ghost. The various telemetry studies in the area often tested Kwewadzsho's frequency just in case. But all was quiet as a moth above a field on a dark night.

By the time school started in September, the wolverine escape was old news. But the kits were never off our minds for long. Through that winter, which was especially cold and hard, we often wondered out loud where they were and what they were doing.

The next spring we had a cleaning frenzy. Everyone pitched in, and we cleaned out the whole research station. Not just the house, but two of the sheds and the garage under our home. Lots of junk went to the transfer station. A lot more was given to people who could use it. We found two computers that had been stored after newer models took their places, and loads of other useful things. One computer went to the Natural Food Coop in town, and the other was set up in a spare room next to our living quarters. I could do all my homework there and called it my office.

When we were done, the station gained two full rooms, a whole shed and part of another, and most of a garage. The halls were no longer crowded with haphazardly stored items and equipment. We were all standing around amazed at how much inconvenience everyone had just grown used to over the years when the FAX machine began to chatter.

Mark went over and glanced at it. Then he let out a long thin whistle and forgot we were there. We crowded around. The message that materialized was from the Auction Office of the Ontario Trappers Association. A wolverine pelt had come in that was almost white. It had not been trapped, but was a road kill that was found just outside of Pickle Lake, Ontario. Mark didn't wait to see what the rest of the letter said about the long trail of contacts that led to the message being directed to him. He slid a drawer open, took out a computer disk, slipped its cardboard jacket off and dashed to his office.

I looked at the disk jacket. In crisp magic marker it said: "Wolverine: Other Journal."

"Nels and I paddled right through Pickle Lake," Mom said. "A road goes there and beyond before it stops somewhere farther north."

Maggie touched the disk jacket.

"Mark mentioned this."

"What is it?"

"It's data and theories and observations he keeps that don't fit into the reports and findings yet. Some of it is just more questions. Also, he said that he keeps stuff in there that would never wash with the scientific community and some of the rigidness there."

I was confused. There was great excitement that glowed right out of Mark and the message, but suddenly I was crying hard. Maggie and Mom scrunched down and held me. It was Maggie's soft husky voice that spoke first.

"You might have named Ghost perfectly. The part of a being that can't and won't die might just keep coming back."

She always knew just what to say. Sometimes the power that flowed all around her made my hair rise and my skin feel cool. Sometimes the darkness of her eyes amazed me.

Days later I had a dream. Not a dream really, because I was awake. Now that I was taking sauna on the top bench where the heat is most intense, I sometimes needed to cool more frequently than the others. I had stepped out one night and stood cooling in the air. I spun myself hard enough so my arms lifted a bit and the stars made long tracks across my eyes. Just as I stopped I felt two heavy paws on my upper chest, the flat part just below the collar bones. I don't know if I thought I really saw, or just knew, that Ghost had come to me, was somehow my size, and said clear as day: "Never forget. Never forget me or anything else."

As we often did after the final heating session in sauna, we accompanied Maggie part way home so we could all take one last swim and say goodnight. This time it was just Mom and Maggie and me.

"Kristin, you came back in like a shooting star. How could you fill the sauna with so much light?"

I knew they knew something, so I told the story. For the first time, it seemed like they felt all excited around me, the way I always felt around them. Sometimes there is so much lightness inside I can't seem to hold it all. I just get radiant, feel expanded past the surface of my skin. I don't quite know how to say so.

Maggie had one of her surprises. "Funny you should have that visit tonight. Mark got a package in the mail today. If you had a choice between the memory of Ghost alive, or to have his pelt, which would you choose? If that isn't too weird."

"I'd like the pelt I guess. I don't think that would bother me. That's what came isn't it?"

"Yes."

Ghost had come home again. We never did swim. Just walked home feeling light and full while the bats whisked over the water snapping up insects. There was just enough light to go without flashlights. Occasionally we'd hear a bat wing hit a leaf or branch among trees along the trail.

Two weeks after summer vacation had started, Maija-Riitta came by - not just to visit. "It's June twenty-first," she announced as if that explained everything.

And maybe it did, because Mom put her hand on my shoulder and said, "Better pay attention."

Maija-Riitta had her cane in one hand and a metal bow saw in the other. Something compact made a small bulge in the front pocket of the green apron she always wore. She must have borrowed some running shoes from one of her grandkids. They were the bulky, gel-filled kind that everyone had, but on an old woman they looked really funny, like she might enter the portage race during the Voyageur Festival, or leap all the way across the Blueberry Fair in a single bound, just to surprise us.

We walked down the trail toward the lake and Maggie's place. Maija-Riitta moved fast for someone her age, and had her eyes up high and down low. She paused twice to stuff some early mushrooms into her pocket. She stopped where some white birch saplings leaned into the trail for better light. "Aha. This is good."

She tapped one of the saplings with her cane and instructed me to cut it down. It was only a few inches in diameter, maybe twenty feet tall. "We need the softest tip-top branches, Kristin. And we need to select for the best leaves on thin long twigs."

Then I knew. We were getting the birch whisks for the sauna. The old ladies called them "vihtas" and we all switched them over our skin to get even more tingly and clean feeling.

Maija-Riitta told me how to get them in early summer when the leaves are still fresh and soft, but late enough so they are firmly attached to the twigs. She drew an old Finnish knife with a wooden sheath from her pocket. It was really sharp.

Together we selected the best branches for the bundles, trimmed them to about twenty inches long, and bound them together with a long, thin branch stripped of leaves and twigs. "Like this. Poke an end right through, then wind it up tight like string. Leave enough to poke the other end through in the opposite direction. That's it, like a staple. No knots."

Then we trimmed the ends smooth on the handle, and lay each finished vihta aside. They smelled heavenly, and even after being dried all year long, that same odor would return every time the vihta was soaked in warm water. Maija-Riitta said she could imagine the whisper of vihtas gently whisking the bodies of sauna takers all over the world. And I could too, sitting there in the sun with our noses pressed to the leaves, inhaling the magic of fresh birch.

"Now we make a small one, for the Tonttu."

Tonttu is the spirit that comes to occupy a well-loved sauna. In ours, there is a peg near the floor in back under the benches. The small vihta hangs there. Someone even made a tiny wooden water bucket and miniature birch ladle, just like the full-sized ones we use, and they stay there too. Maija-Riitta said it wouldn't hurt to leave a little bread or cheese for the Tonttu, because even if the Tonttu wasn't hungry, a deer mouse might be.

We hung the vihtas to dry in the sauna on a

string stretched between two nails. Before leaving me to have tea with Mom, Maija-Riitta put the bow saw in a corner and her knife on the windowsill. "Always remember, about June twenty-first, that's the best time."

The next day I went back by myself and made four more vihtas. Just to make sure I could do it right. Whenever I carried that knife in my pocket, it felt like there was nothing in the world that I couldn't take care of. And it's a good thing too, because later Mom saw the knife there on the windowsill and touched it and said, "Well, I see you have another responsibility."

I sat up straight then.

Another summer and fall went by. I fit into the research projects more naturally, not even realizing it was unusual for a 14-year-old to have so much experience in the woods, and so much responsibility at a job. Mark and Mom paid me, because although I was helpful, I couldn't be an official government employee.

Early in winter another package arrived from Canada – this time from Quebec. Mark was even more excited than last time. It contained Kwewadzsho's radio collar, a letter, and a sheaf of papers that were photocopies of reports from lots of different people. Some were in French and Mark sent them to the Language Department at the University in the Twin Cities to be translated.

Kwewadzsho had slipped her collar near a place called Wemindji, almost directly east across James Bay from where the Attawapiskat River enters. Mark still couldn't know if Kwewadzsho had crossed the ice or followed the land around the southern end of the bay. It would be two hundred kilometers across, more than five hundred around – to us, more than 100 miles across, and about 300 miles around. But given the overall distance she had traveled, it hardly mattered.

The shed collar was discovered by caribou hunters who found it on the ice in a heap of heads, lower legs, and paunches left by other hunters. Wolf tracks, and the one set of wolverine tracks, showed at least several days' worth of scavenging.

The returned collar was remarkable enough, but it was the photocopies that made Mark's excitement shoot right off the scale.

"He's impossible when he's this excited," Roberta said. "I'm going to move in with you guys until he calms down."

Each page was a report of tracks. The fur buyers pooled them from hunters scattered all over, and from hearsay, and even from a helicopter pilot who saw strange tracks on a lake and actually landed on the ice to see what the unfamiliar prints might be.

Mark put one of Nels' maps on the wall and stuck a red pin at each of the locations reported on the photocopies. Even without the eavesdropping of the radio-collar transmissions, the gradual printing of wolverine tracks across Quebec was impressive.

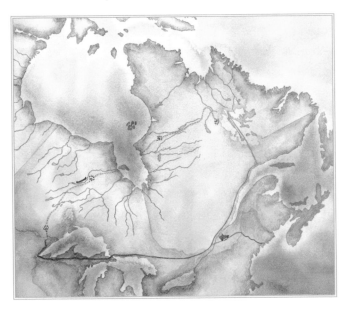

There were no better observers of sign than the Cree hunters who were sprinkled over that vast land all winter. Most had never seen wolverine tracks in their lives, only heard of them from older hunters. Yet there was a name in Cree: ᖴᐃᐦᖴᐦᐲᒉᑯᐤ and with only minor dialectic differences, the same in Naskapi and Montagnais, too: ᖴᐃᐦᐸᑯᐤ

Even as Mark stuck pins in his map and waited for the translations from French, the two-way radios that linked the winter bush camps together chattered endlessly about the tracks crossing everyone's territories. There might have been a very old native hunter or two drumming and dreaming, trying to see into the meaning of these new tracks. And every new set was excitedly approached by the hunters as they moved across the land, checking their snares and fish sets, or following the caribou, or searching for ptarmigan in the willows.

Mark's pins traveled up the Grand Riviere de la Baliene, past the impossible maze of islands, peninsulas, and bays of Lac Bienville, then over a height of land, toward any of a half dozen rivers that ran into the Riviere Caniapiscau. Then, in a huge mix of barren ridges, sprawling lakes, and tumbling rivers in wooded valleys, all news stopped.

Kwewadzsho had left the Cree territories and had reached the land of the Naskapi and a few of the farther flung Montagnais families. Mark was ecstatic. Although Kwewadzsho had slipped her collar, and even though she might have followed the Pons or the Serigny or the Riviere du Mort — River of Death, Mark was sure she was alive and well and on her way. Where she was going, or why, who could possibly know?

Mark paced and talked all during our Saturday supper together and all during the sauna afterwards. He was so worked up that he had to go out and cool off twice as often as the rest of us. He barged back in already talking again.

"It's uncanny, Mari. You read a book about the Naskapi and learn a word. You name an animal born in captivity of parents who were born in a zoo. The animal escapes, makes a beeline for Naskapi country thousands of miles away, somehow travels to the far side of one of the biggest bays in the world, sneaks around hydro projects, roads, towns, and thousands of traps. And keeps going. Randomly, we know some of what she has been doing. You tell me. What comes first? Does she know her name? Is she following some odd destiny? I'm supposed to be a scientist, and I've turned into a stark raving mystic. For all I know, that darn creature snuck into Nels' books and read Cabot for herself before striking off to Labrador. Probably read your trip notes for the most direct route to Attawapiskat too."

Mark slumped onto his spot on the bench, and

for some reason we all began to laugh. We got laughing so hard we couldn't stop, and it kept coming in waves and peals. Every time Mark waved his arms helplessly, we laughed harder, until we had to go outside to breathe. In some way, I knew there was magic in the world as surely as there was air in our lungs. We looked up at the Big Dipper, and as if there were no other possible thought, wondered where, under that great ladle and its attendant North Star, Kwewadzsho was and what she might be doing.

Back inside, Mark the scientist did a surprising thing. He had never dedicated the splash of water to stone before, but there was no mistaking this. "Pisssshhhhh..." said the water greeting superheated stone.

"Here's to the lovely Kwewadzsho."

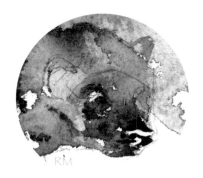

The seasons rolled by. Nels and Mom planned another trip, this one in winter. Mom was eager to learn more about toboggans and long-distance snowshoe travel. She and Nels felt ready to experience the hunting and ice fishing they had studied about while devouring a book about the traditional native skills and that was full of practical information.

In winter I would be in school, so I knew I couldn't go on the trip. Maggie was going to stay with me again, but she seemed distant and a little sad. No one said anything, but I wished I knew what to do. Both of us longed to be going on this trip, and I suppose that was troubling her.

When the time came, Mom and Nels drove to Quebec City and on along the North Shore of the St. Lawrence. In Sept-Iles they boarded the Quebec North Shore & Labrador Railway. Two hundred and eighty-six miles up the line they got out at a place called Esker, where Nels had started and finished a number of trips. That is how we learned more of Kwewadzsho.

How I wished I'd been with them as the stories unfolded!

When Mom and Nels were unloading their gear from the baggage car that night, they met a young Montagnais hunter who spoke a little English. He was picking up a hundred gallons of gas, and noticed the toboggans.

"You speak hinglish?" he asked, approaching Mom.

"Oui, bonjour, not much French."

"I see people with toboggan every year. You know Peetair and Aleeyson? They write book. My fren."

"Yes, we read their book. We don't know Peter and Alyson, only know of them."

"Come wif me. My camp two miles. I pull you sleds my machine. Then come back for you. Walk da way you see dis red light go." He patted the taillight of his Ski-Doo with a big embroidered mitten trimmed with marten fur.

Nels helped roll the two drums of fuel onto the flat sled being towed behind the Ski-Doo. After the fuel was lashed down securely, Nels and the young hunter hitched the two toboggans on behind, tied side by side so they wouldn't tip over.

It wasn't long before Mom and Nels could see the lone headlight bobbing in the drifts as machine and driver headed back to pick them up. Mom got on behind the driver and Nels rode in the sled behind. A few miles later, when the machine pulled off the lake onto an island. the headlight swept across a cluster of tents. Two were regular wall tents, the kind you could buy ready-made at The Northern. The third was huge, made of big rolls of canvas pitched over a loaf-shaped framework of poles. There were two stovepipes poking through the roof of that one, and everyone was inside.

It was toasty warm from the two barrel stoves, and candles cast a lovely soft light. The young hunter turned out to be Jean-Marie McKenzie. His mother was the oldest woman in the group and seemed to be in charge of the big tent. There were a few other relatives who were staying in the two smaller tents.

Everyone was very quiet. They just sipped tea together, so Mom and Nels smiled a lot and accepted some bannock and dried caribou meat. After a while, with no goodnights or comments, people went to their own tents, and Jean-Marie indicated that Mom and Nels were to roll out their sleeping bags near the second stove.

Mom and Nels thought this was a very convenient first night of their trip because they didn't have to make their own camp in the dark in a strange place. But it turned out that another big surprise would be waiting in the morning. Over tea just after sunrise, Jean-Marie made a special invitation. "My mudder. Me too. Want to know you stay wif us?"

Mom and Nels looked at each other, surprised, each knowing the other would never miss such an amazing opportunity. They nodded enthusiastically and said "Yes" about twenty times.

They pitched their tent and stove where Jean-Marie suggested, and everyone helped lay a thick, lovely floor of black spruce boughs like the other tents had. The original trip plans were abandoned and the serendipitous two weeks in the McKenzie camp were splendid beyond belief. Mom and Nels learned more than they had ever dared hope for, and were incorporated into whatever was going on as if it weren't unusual at all for two strangers to appear off the train and be adopted. People just went about their work and anyone could be included or not as they wished. Always there was a lot of relaxing in the big tent. The whole group gathered there for meals, tea, and talking.

As the friendships blossomed and everyone became comfortable with each other, Mom asked a question. "You know Kwewadzsho?" She hoped she had pronounced it right and knew right away she had it close enough.

"Kwewadzsho? You know Kwewadzsho?" Jean-Marie asked with widened eyes. Then he talked with his mother in Montagnais, and at length she nodded. He told a story.

"One year ago I dream. I see Kwewadzsho come over a ridge from de west. My fadder's hunting ground is dat way. Maybe it is heem coming. Maybe not. He dead long time. Five year, maybe more. Next day I go on machine up river to check traps. I have lynx trap set in t'ick trees where de big river comes into Menikwa from west. Farder up all traps for Wabstan, pine marten. I see somet'ing beeg, not caught so good. I stop machine. Walk. It looks at me. Kwewadzsho. I say it out loud, soft, over and over. It looks at me. Beeg, beeg, powerful, but it not move. Looks calm. Looks at me. It don't jump or fight, gets low, lets a beeg air out. Breath, you know? Waits. I talk to it all along. Soft. Don't move fast. Somet'ing make me not kill Kwewadzsho. Ver strange.

"Only one foot caught. T'ree toes only. Caught only short time, no struggle. I talk, it stays ver quiet. Looks at me. I t'row coat over it, put snowshoe over coat and pull so only caught toes show. Kwewadzsho never fight, never move. I spring trap hoping he not mad, not fight me. Ver strong him.

"I pick up snowshoe, coat. Kwewadzsho stay quiet, looks at me ver hard, ver close. He not run. Walks slowly short way, stops and looks. I toss him frozen fish from my bag.

"When Kwewadzsho gone, I look at tracks close. Wabush, rabbit, he hop into trap by mistake, big problem, get caught. Kwewadzsho find rabbit. He pulls, chews rabbit, pushes and chews to get rabbit. Cuts rabbit in half. But one foot pushing on trap, trap closes on foot when rabbit cut. Then me. He not scared me. He lets me give him free."

And Mom and Nels told Jean-Marie their long tale. Jean-Marie translated to his mother. Talk flowed and looped and ran. At one point Jean-Marie said, "Dreams ver important. Never forget, always tell."

Back in Minnesota, Maggie and I were a little blue for a while, but still we had a great time. She practiced fiddle while I did homework. Sometimes we'd rent movies, and she taught me to appreciate the strange pace and complexity of foreign films. Maggie was even more demanding and firm than Mom in some ways, but in other ways we were like pirates, breaking the rules and having fun.

When Mom and Nels returned, it took several suppers and saunas to get the full run of stories. Mark was amazed. He went to the map and put a red pin where the McPhadyen River entered Menihek Lake. It looked like Kwewadzsho had headed east from Lac Bienville and reached the Caniapiscau River. A range of high hills on the east side stretched more than a hundred miles north and south. Kwewadzsho must have turned south, upstream, and crossed a lake-filled labyrinth west of the hills until she crossed a low pass and encountered the first big river that cut to the east – the McPhadyen, which led to the McKenzie territories on Menihek.

In looking through the reference books again, all sorts of McKenzies showed up in and around the central Labrador Plateau. The book where Mom had learned the word "kwewadzsho" had pictures of various McKenzie family members. And the new winter skills book Mom and Nels liked so well had a picture of Jean-Marie himself – snowshoeing, with a traditional game bag on his back. It was as if a great weaver was busy braiding many separate trails together. That thought gave me a splendid thrill, but even then I never suspected that the weaver was busy still.

Maggie couldn't get the Kwewadzsho stories out of her head. "This is big," she said. "Something's gonna happen. We all have to get back there somehow."

We kept gathering around the maps in the evenings, and one time Mom looked up at us clustered on the floor and grinned. "Oh no," she said. "The map disease is contagious."

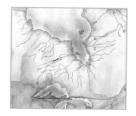

During high school I could tell life was speeding up. The summers didn't seem as long anymore, especially after I started leading canoe trips at Camp Jiimaan on the edge of town. I was determined to stay on the staff until I was 18 so that I could lead one of the summer-long trips to James or Hudson Bay.

During my last summer at camp, Mark's funding for Maggie's salary was not renewed. While he was looking for another source, Maggie free-lanced on a crew doing seabird research in Alaska during the

short Arctic breeding season. Then she landed another job that she could do on her way back from Alaska, studying birds of prey in the Snake River Canyon in Idaho.

I was busy and distracted with camp responsibilities and being "on trail." I only thought of her once in a while, like when I was swimming under the stars, or at banquet when we had fiddle music. Then I'd get a strange, powerful, achy feeling that would last for days.

That was the summer after senior year, and it was a good one. I did get to co-lead a trip to Hudson Bay for the camp, one of two Bay Trips that went that year. I had a choice of the Seal River in Manitoba, or the Thlewiaza in what is now Nunavut, but was then the Northwest Territories. I chose the Thlewiaza because it was farther north, and the Northwest Territories were spoken of in hushed, mythical whispers among those older campers and staff who finally made it to "The Bay." Around camp, even Heaven or Hell were regarded as not very interesting destinations compared to "The North" or "The Bay," the absolute fuel and fire of our canoeing dreams and passions.

I was in town at the end of the season when someone at the Post Office said they'd seen Maggie's truck. I suddenly realized how much I'd missed her, and it didn't seem fair that someone else had seen her first. But it was all ok again when we were all together. With Maggie back everything felt like a snug family reunion after a big disruption. We would bring a pot of tea to the swimming ledges to hear about her adventures in Alaska and Idaho, and I'd tell stories about my Thlewiaza trip. Maggie really was an exciting big sister to me.

I didn't go to college right away. Mom and Nels had arranged to stay in the Labrador bush with Jean-Marie McKenzie all winter, and Maggie suggested that I join them because college would be ready for me any time, and the stay with a native family wouldn't be. When Nels and Mom said I could join them, I couldn't believe my excitement. First the Bay trip, now this. Mom was right a long time ago when she said, "When the time is right, we'll travel there. We can't help ourselves."

Mark had found another funding source for Maggie. I was hoping she could come with us anyway, but she'd already signed the contract, and she said Mark wouldn't be able to replace her if she walked out on it. But while we were talking about it, she pulled me aside. She had an intensity and earnestness about her that I could feel but not read.

"Kristin, sometimes I don't think you know how lucky you are. Everyone around you makes stuff happen, or at least tries to steer things into happening. You're that way too, a lot of the time, because it comes naturally, grows out of your surroundings. But most people are not that fortunate. They have to work harder, and jump through hoops, and claw their way to the best opportunities. And then only if they recognize them in the first place. For some, that's the hardest part.

"You have to pay attention to anything and everything on this trip. You won't have any way of knowing in advance what a magnificent thing this is, and what might be rare and unbelievably

valuable. Learn everything you can. Don't judge —
it gets in the way of learning. Watch hard. You'll be
way out on a limb culturally, how you view the
world, what you think you know or believe. Try
everything - language, physical skills, and don't be
afraid of mistakes. You can be free from the
burden of needing to be right all the time because
no one there will know or care. Keep a very full
journal - write about everything. If you need to
jump-start it, write it as a letter to me. I can't tell
you how envious I am, jealous even."

She was holding both my shoulders and her dark
eyes had a fierceness that made me determined to
never ever let her down. This was not a question
or a suggestion. The seriousness made me tingle
with something like fear, and my own voice seemed
small and not very capable of much.

"I'll try, Maggie. I'll really, really try."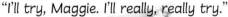

During the fall, after Camp Jiimaan was buttoned up for the winter and while we were getting ready for the trip, I took a job in town as a waitress. I shared the floor with Betsy Sååskilampi who was in her sixties and knew everything about the world. She got tips as if she were some kind of queen nobody could do without. Shannon, a girl my age who just came on for the busy hours Friday and Saturday evenings, wore clothes that made the most of her boobs and bottom, and hair that was all puff and in the way. She was outraged that her take of tips never even came close to Betsy's haul. "She's like nothin' but somebody's friggin' grandmother. What's the deal?"

True enough. But Betsy really knew how to flirt, and who with, and when she needed to be no-nonsense. She could read everyone from the minute they walked in, and she could be a saint, a mother, an aunt, a confidant, or a tease, with unerring accuracy and no shred of insincerity.

I never really got it, and tried to hide behind a bland smiley mask that I hoped wouldn't radiate much. Twice Betsy was there for me when men made passes at me. One guy even stayed outside until closing time, and that scared me. I could coach and lead people down complicated rapids and chase bears away from our food up north, but I couldn't seem to hold my own in the middle of town in a public place that was supposedly safe.

And I couldn't stop the angry tears that soaked Betsy's solid shoulders, even though I was sure I was much too old for them. What a relief to finish up at the end of October.

I really would miss Betsy, and made a point of eating breakfast at the restaurant occasionally when it was her early morning shift and the place was not very crowded – just the folks who get about early and are interesting. I always liked their practical banter and opinions. If it were a slow morning, Betsy would sit with me and sip coffee. She knew I liked tea, and always served it in the blue and white Finnish flag mugs that said SISU.

RM

A few weeks before Thanksgiving we headed off, packed to the roof with gear. I was glued to the window as soon as things were unfamiliar. Before we left, Maggie gave me two books. One was a hardbound Grumbacher empty book with quality sketching paper to be used for a journal, and the other was the pocket sized Dictionnaire Larousse Francais-Anglais et Anglais-Francais.

She held both my hands and kissed me goodbye on the lips. That intense look was on her face again, maybe so I wouldn't forget anything she said. Hours later I thought maybe I'd sensed a troubling wistfulness, and I was afraid I might never know the meaning of it. But then I realized it was just that we'd been apart so much in the past months, and we were sad about missing each other again for a while.

We would be gone through March, maybe even into April. Already the trip was becoming adventurous. East of Quebec City at Baie St. Catherine, the road stopped at the edge of a huge tidal river mouth - the Saguenay. A ferry that was just part of the highway with no fee took us across to Tadoussac where the road continued. We saw Fin and Minke whales in the St. Lawrence right from the road.

When we arrived in Sept-Iles on a Wednesday afternoon, we arranged our gear and loaded it onto boxcar number 36508. Early the next morning we were among the crowd at the passenger gate of the Quebec North Shore & Labrador Railroad. I had never been on a train before, and this was nothing like the Amtrak trains in Minnesota. It was a mix of freight and passenger cars and had such a magical sounding name. When we headed north into the bush, we completely left behind the world we knew.

The whole experience of the winter was incredible beyond anything I could have imagined, but the most remarkable part happened during the last week of our stay. It's the only part I can tell with clarity. The rest is still unfolding as intricately as a dream, and only slowly coming into focus and gaining meaning.

It was April, and the top few inches of snow were soft on a sunny day. We were west of Menihek Lake, coming home with three caribou in the sleds behind the snow machines. On the settled spring snow we could go almost anywhere, so we unhitched the sleds to zoom up to a barren ridge top and enjoy the view. Looking back the way we'd come, we could see the lakes dotted with creamy brown and white caribou. To the east Menihek stretched its eighty-mile length north and south. Way off we could see other hunters, their snow machines like tiny bugs on the huge white surface.

Just as we were ready to descend, a line of tracks caught our attention. They were big. Fresh. Printed so clearly in the thawing snow that we could see the wrinkles in the pads in every track. Each print had a perfect crescent of five magnificent claws. No one spoke.

When we stood to look in the direction where the tracks vanished, we were huddled close. We just looked and looked. There was no language we could mold for that long view of a big world under a bright sky, and the single line of tracks that had somehow brought us all to this moment. We broke apart but still lingered. The tracks came up over a curve of hill and vanished over a curve of hill. We always seemed to be tangent to them, wondering, watching, listening, hoping for something we could never quite define enough to even mention.

After hitching up the freight sleds to continue back to camp, Jean-Marie looked back at the ridge. "Ah, Kwewadzsho. Like d'ese hills. Stay. Ver happy, me."

All the way back to camp I could sense why years of connections seemed so much more fulfilling than short answers. I thought of the card Mom had given me the year I became a young woman. "Never leave the trail of curiosity for long. Never abandon your personal path because a friend or a teacher or the system expects you to. Never stop dreaming." I kept that card because I didn't know what it meant. Now every year it means more and more. I think Mom gave it to me to discover. Like the contents of a tool kit, or Maggie's watercolors.

I was too excited to write much in my journal that night. My hand would get shaking too much whenever I thought of that whole day. All I was able to say in big blocky letters was this: "Maggie — we saw her tracks. I touched them!"

There was a sudden change of pace the day we were to catch the southbound train. We packed up and had the sled all loaded for the trip to Esker at mile 286. Although Canada had been metric for years, the QNS& L never switched to kilometers. A white sign with the mileage was posted every mile along the tracks on the poles that held the wires. There were twenty poles per mile and each one had a small metal number telling the mileage and the pole number. You always knew just where you were along the tracks.

It was a mild day with no wind and we didn't have to wait long. The family that was camped near mile 308 on the line radioed us to say the train had just arrived there. It was actually on time. Usually we'd have to wait for hours if we were picking someone up, or retrieving supplies and gear sent up from the Reserve. The train almost always appeared on the right day - north on Thursdays, south on Fridays - we just never knew what time it would come.

We made the few miles to trackside with forty minutes to spare. The whole camp made the trip to see us off, even those we were not sure liked us or cared that we were there. We'd become closest to the older people and the youngest kids, and they hugged us hard and gave us the stylized quick kiss on each cheek. We were not the only ones crying.

It was like an axe falling. How could such an overwhelming part of our life be severed so cleanly? With such finality? In the still, spring air we could hear the throbbing approach of the train for ten minutes. Then it was there. In less than a minute our gear was flung to the baggage handlers and we jumped aboard. Then we were gone. Late November to early April chopped off, just that fast.

It was a good thing the train ride south took so long. We needed time to make the transition from our present-tense life in the bush to the lives we left in November and would return to in a few days. For months we had been in charge of our world, completely dependent on our tiny band, and selectively removed from all the stuff of towns.

We had been predators, as hungry as the foxes, wolves, and gyr falcons that so excited us. Every day we would pull lake trout and pike from nets under the ice or from big hooks on set-lines. All the girls and women in camp had snares for snowshoe hares. The snares were set around the camp and along the trails to firewood and the fish sets. A ten-year-old boy taught me to hunt ptarmigan with a cheap but functional twelve gauge single shot shotgun made in Brazil. When the caribou came, we were busy in a big way. Even Mom learned to use a rifle.

Almost everything we did concerned food. We had huge boxes full of bought stuff. Flour, tea, salt, rice, and oatmeal. And plenty of five-gallon tins of vegetable shortening. The rest was wild food. I knew where it came from, knew how to cut it up and prepare it. Knew it didn't come easy much of the time. And before the caribou came, I got really tired of lake trout.

All winter various extended family members would come and go at the camp. At times there were as many as fifteen people there. We really meshed with the older ones and the pre-school kids. The elders were always busy at something, and we were eager to learn from them and to help out. Often our attempts at learning were funny because we had so little language ability, and methods of teaching and learning were so different from what we were used to. We laughed together a lot. And it was funny because Nels was always doing "women's work," and Mom and I were just as eager with some of the "men's work."

There was a little friction and jealousy among people who were close to my age, or to Mom's and Nels's age. They didn't do anything. Just lay around in the way listening to their CD players. They didn't get wood or water, and would only hunt some of the time. There was always alcohol and who knows what kind of drugs around when they were in camp. They didn't like the attention their parents were giving us, or the affection their children showed us. But they didn't even take care of their own kids. The grandparents were raising the children, in addition to doing all the other work.

I know I'm from liberal folks, but the level of acceptance, non-judgment, and non-interference among our hosts seemed extreme even to me. It's tiring to be that tolerant. When I would think someone was an irresponsible, lazy, good-for-nothing drunk, their people would shrug and say, "too bad, sick," as if there was no such thing as taking responsibility or helping out with the work. It drove me crazy.

Mom said that generation was culturally sick, not in control of anything. They were victims of being neither fully Innu, nor mainstream Quebec. The elders had spent half their formative years on the land before the government made everyone come to the Reserves in the late 1950's and 60's. They knew the taste of freedom and all about the work that earns it. Since they raised the grandkids, the kids at least sense that joy and balance. They don't become lost until television and white-style school systems poison them, and the government dole and hydro settlements teach them there's no need to work at anything. Much of that free money goes to the worst western culture has to offer – junk food, drugs, alcohol, and a lot of stuff nobody needs.

It finally became clear to me how unusual Jean-Marie was. He is right between my age and Mom's age. He should be part of what Mom calls "the lost generation," but he is not. His father brought him to the bush, and he didn't spend so much time in school on the Reserve. Now he is a respected hunter, a "na bow" or even a "mista na bow" - literally "big man." He speaks the native Innu language and French fluently, and English quite well, and he has become a natural leader. I even had kind of a crush on him because he was so kind and competent, funny, and nice. And we really needed him because he was the one with the most English, so he could let us know what was going on and fix our mix-ups and mistakes.

After a winter with my special trip name of Amber, I would have to learn to be Kristin again. The Innu couldn't quite manage an "R" sound after a "K." I was everything from *Cah Lis Teen* to *Little Mali (Mari)*, until Nels suggested they use Amber. They had no trouble with that, although it came out *Ahm Bear*. When we jumped on the train I became Kristin again, without a plan or anyone saying so. It just happened.

One passenger car was almost empty since we were still so close to the north end of the line. We each took our own window seat to watch and think, and to sift back into ourselves after such a long time in a communal camp setting. After a while Mom came and sat with me, and we leaned on each other quietly for a while. Then she passed me her journal, opened to an entry she had made early in our stay.

Today there were lessons in blood. I thought of Diana, goddess of the hunt, wanting to know more about her.

A long time ago I gave birth to a daughter I love as a most beautiful being. Today I killed a beautiful creature twice as heavy as myself. A caribou. Everything went as well as could be. One well-placed shot at close range severed the spine at the base of the head. Then the heart-slamming paradox of horror and relief – relief that death had come quickly without wounding and prolonged struggling, horror that I had killed such a wild and wonderful being. Some of the caribou, even when taken down with a heart and lung shot, ran for quite a ways, and even after falling, their legs would still be trying to run. This was different from taking fish or ptarmigan. This creature has eyes like mine, even lashes. It is big. The females nurse their young. The organs are arranged like mine.

There was solemn quiet when we approached the fallen animal. Jean-Marie and an older uncle, Gregoire, gave me time to touch the ears and muzzle and cry a bit before they got down to the business of removing the innards, saving the heart and the lacey net of fat that surrounds the stomach. Their hands were practiced and efficient, as gentle as a doctor's might be. They paused to show me what to do, where to cut, how to pull and spill the vitals on the snow. This last plunging of hands into the inner heat and smell was my prayer of thanksgiving, a plea for forgiveness, a promise to treat this sacrifice well.

Jean-Marie put his hand on my shoulder at just the right moment. He didn't say anything, but that touch through the folds of heavy winter clothes was just what I needed. I was shaking.

I felt a strange surge of simultaneous humility and pride as the snowmobiles pulled into camp, each towing several caribou. Even Nels, who had hunted deer in Minnesota, was quiet and somber. The numbers were so remarkable. This land is huge, and in winter it's starkly white, green, and blue. It looks empty. Much of the time it is empty. Then this morning a band of thirty caribou speckled the far reach of lake ice. They moved on, but more and more followed. Groups of ten, fifty, and a hundred or more were streaming out of the northwest like an unstoppable tide. By afternoon there were scattered bands everywhere we looked, and thousands had passed.

It had all started during breakfast with a single short word. Genevieve had stepped out to get water from the hole chiseled in the ice. She popped her head back in too soon for the bucket to have been filled and said, "Atik."

The big main tent emptied so fast we couldn't believe it. By the time we managed to join everyone at the lake edge, some of the men were already gassing up machines, stuffing bullets in their pockets, pulling on insulated overpants, and strapping rifles across their backs or stowing them along the running boards of the snowmobiles.

Gregoire directed the hunters to two islands, about a mile apart, where some caribou would pass. Suddenly, all the practice sighting in the rifle with Nels was going to involve something other than a piece of firewood stuck up in the snow as a target. I was scared. I tried to review everything. I visualized the crease behind the shoulder for a heart and lungs shot, and the base of the head where a shot would sever the spine if it were at close range. Then we were behind our island, waiting with Jean-Marie and Gregoire. A string of seventeen caribou came closer and closer. I don't even remember pushing the safety off - or the reports of our rifles.

A few intense hours after the first sighting, we were back in camp with nine caribou. We had tea as soon as we returned, with no mention of the hunt. Respect again. Afterwards, Gregoire looked up at the older women around the stove. He said only a few soft words, and pointed toward the snowmobiles in the Innu way, not with a finger or hand gesture, but by pursing his lips and pointing them in the direction beyond the tent wall. They put on their shawls and coats and grabbed their knives. There was meat in camp. Work to be done. An ancient balance between feast and famine had just tipped to the feast side. Subtle joy among our hosts.

The two-way radio in the tent crackled with news all day and evening. As the caribou moved down the lakes and rivers and ridges, snowmobiles from the families and camps south of us moved up to meet them. Other camps far to the east were making ready to travel west.

Late that night I was cold from going out to pee, and staying too long watching the northern lights. Back inside I snuggled my sleeping bag up close to Nels and burrowed partly into his, so I could listen to his heart through his longjohn top. It was beating so slowly in sleep. It amazed me how estranged my culture is from sustenance, food, and love of the bigger world so full of real connections. Here we are as adults, just catching on to what any Innu child knows implicitly, completely, without anyone filling the world with too many words.

There was a loose page inserted that Mom must have written later.

Mrs. McKenzie is going to guide me through the working of the hides and smoke-tanning. The mittens I make for Kristin and Nels will hold love and life, and what I used to assume was violence. All this new knowledge to cradle warm hands. I think now that predator and prey are not in opposition, not the flip sides of a coin. They – we, really – are on the same side, we share a pact, a responsibility, the root of which is survival. This is hard for me to grasp.

I read that entry a couple of times before handing it back. Mom was leaning close, reading along. The black spruce and snowy bogs flew by the window, as if the train were holding still and the landscape itself was fleeing to the north.

"It's hard to know just what we learned all winter, isn't it?" Mom commented.

"Yeah, Mom," I said, feeling a bit uneasy, "and that's not all. You know those first mittens you made? " She nodded and I went on.

"I hate to tell you this now, but I gave them to a woman who flew in when the ski-plane with the government nurse visited. She had left hers at the last stop, and there were lots more camps to visit. I wish I had them, now that I know what they meant to you." For a second she looked disappointed, but then she brightened.

"Don't worry," she said. "You still have the important part. And whoever you gave them to needed them. We have such odd attachments to things. It's not important. What's important is that you gave them to who needed them most. That's community, the way caring works. You did the best thing."

It was a relief to hear some English being spoken on the train, and a number of people asked us about what we'd been up to. I tried to imagine what lay ahead. What we would be re-entering. Even so, I was completely unprepared for the train emerging from the Moise River canyon into the lights of Sept-Iles. The bustle of the train yard was chaotic and organized all at once. French, English, and the Innu languages filled the air. The pushing and shoving and sudden activity all had desperate intent and direction.

Just as suddenly, all was quiet. In less than half an hour, the station was empty. Pickup trucks full of caribou and gear headed off toward the two local Reserves — one in town and one up the road in Maliotenam. Taxis vanished. Cars were gone. The train was silent and dark.

Although the temperature was far warmer here than in the interior plateau country, the moist air off the St. Lawrence seemed thick and shivery. The ice was gone from the river, and the snow had melted except for the plowed banks along the roads and edges of parking lots. We had left winter twelve hours earlier when we boarded the train, and got off in the thicker air of thaw and moisture and springtime.

We looked at the lights of our own culture as if we were stranded tourists from another planet. It was more than overwhelming. I felt stunned, almost sick.

On the drive to the motel the glare and brightness of town really got to me. It was scary seeing it so fresh. And I was unsettled by something on the train too. Toward the end of the run, when fatigue had set in and the cars were blue with cigarette smoke, I had slept a little. Not well. I was stretched between sadness to be leaving and amazement at all that had happened. After dark, with the view gone and no way to keep track of the mileage marks, I slept harder. I dreamed of Ghost again. It may have been the sound of the train coming through, but Ghost and I ran and ran. We ran so long and hard and frantically that we couldn't breathe. I didn't know what the rush was, and sometimes Ghost was Maggie, then Ghost again. We were not getting anywhere and I awoke troubled. A vague fear finally settled into wondering what had come over Maggie during the month before we left and why I hadn't thought more of it at the time. She was restless in the blinds, and a stiffness took the grace from her stride. She never commented, but some light left her eyes every time she pushed her fists into the small of her back to arch and stretch.

Later, in a motel in Sept-Iles, we tried to call home. It was hard to believe we had been out of touch for five months. There was no answer at our place where Maggie was staying, and the answering machine never even clicked on. Nels thought a minute and decided to call Mark and Roberta. They might be up, since it was an hour earlier in Minnesota. When Nels made it through, his excitement suddenly folded up around him. He didn't talk much and we saw him slump in shocked silence. He just listened for a long time. At the end all he said was, "OK, thanks."

He tried not to choke, put the receiver down. Mom and I were frozen. Had not breathed. Could not imagine.

"Maggie's surprised us again. She's gone. Mark says she didn't feel well. She really ached. The cancer turned up in her bones. After chemotherapy and radiation, there was nothing more to be done. She was ready to go into hospice care at the hospital if necessary, but hoped Mark and Roberta could keep her home. They agreed to try, and her last days went pretty fast without much need for painkillers. Her last four days were really bad. She couldn't move or talk. They turned her every two hours and changed her bed all the time, and packed pillows so her skin wouldn't get sore spots and her joints wouldn't ache so much.

"Early her last morning she made a sound that woke them, and they held her hands until her last breath came out in a long easy sigh.

"She died at the beginning of March when the light was coming back. She left us all letters we can read when we get there. She...she..." Nels' eyes were getting wet and his mouth had a little twitch as he tried to finish repeating what Mark had told him on the phone. "I hope she knew how much we loved her. They'll tell us the details... when... we... home."

There wasn't much sleep that night. We could hear each other crying quietly and tossing. Sometimes Mom would come and hold me like I was still a little girl. Sometimes she and Nels held each other. Once, very late, they went to the shower and I heard the water running. I guess they found a way to quench some despair by loving each other there.

Somehow we got home. Driving in a daze, sleeping poorly, driving more, sleeping again. At one point Nels banged on the steering wheel.

Mom gently put her hand on his leg and answered as if he'd said something out loud. "We'll never have an answer. It just keeps us wondering, and reminds us to live hard and well, with nothing taken for granted."

When we saw Maggie's truck, we fell apart again, and Mark, Roberta, and Amanda had all they could do to hold us up and welcome us home.

The next week there was a ceremony. Only a few of Maggie's family attended, and some of her friends — the ones who couldn't travel to be here — sent letters. It was all sad. There was a person who claimed to be the mother, but didn't seem to care. There were two brothers who were estranged from each other, and a sister who was not a sister to the brothers. They all seemed surprised at the amount of love that poured out of Maggie's friends from here. Mostly they complained about the drive from the airport in Duluth, and how crummy it was staying at the cheapest motel in town. They didn't even have their own plans for her ashes, and left them with her "family" here. We put them under the sauna and at the swimming ledges. The strangeness of Maggie's family deepened our sadness. We longed to know the unknowable.

When they all left and I was alone in Maggie's truck for the first time, I read her letter to me. It was brief. Maybe she waited too long and had to conserve her fading energy.

Dear Kristin,

I'll be leaving soon. I don't want to. I'm not afraid anymore. It will be easier with you being gone. You won't see me reduced to a baggy shell that can't move. Sudden news is easier than slow wasting. You'll have to believe me.

I suppose it will surprise you to hear that I learned a lot from you. It's always a surprise when young friends find out from older friends that learning goes both ways. You are like a sister. (I had a half sister, but I never got to know her.) You are my friend, and I

hope you don't mind if I say you are like a daughter,
if ever I'd wished for one. And I did when I met you.
Slowly, you will come to know how much love I felt for
you. It takes time and all the windings of the trails we
travel. I'd like you to have my truck.

Keep your dreams close to your heart. I'll visit you
if I can, but I don't know. See that my fiddle and bow
are given to whoever is just right. That's where my
voice will stay. Learn to dance.

Love, Maggie

I wanted more. I wanted words that would tell me
why she left me, that would make sense of her
death, that would take her place. I ached and cried
and threw things. I slept all day and couldn't sleep
at night. I turned numb. And when I finally had a few
moments of feeling better, I felt guilty. Eventually, it
all settled down to a great, sad longing.

Having Maggie's truck provided some solace. It
was almost as if she could continue to talk to me.
There was such care in how the camper part was
built, and so much of her quirky wonderful
brightness in it.

I listened to her music collection there, reclined
on her bunk. She liked the recorded music well
enough, but I recalled how excitedly she spoke of
playing along, or dancing for real, while the

fiddles, banjo, and maybe a hammered dulcimer rang out. And one of those flat Celtic drums drove the band and held the whole dance hall to a common heartbeat.

Above the bunk there were dome lights I could aim for reading, and I saw a slight mismatch in the grain of a panel next to them. I poked that piece and it shifted. I slid it, and a little compartment opened up. A bunch of letters were in there. Two were love letters - achingly beautiful love letters both written at the time of a parting of ways. The date of the most recent one meant she came to us broken hearted, and I never knew. I had been so excited by new friendship I forgot to listen to her more, or better, or whatever it would have taken. Maybe I was too young then anyway.

But Mom had known everything. They had talked often and late, after I had gone to sleep. I did recall hearing Mom comforting Maggie a few times while she tried to muffle great heaving sobs, so as not to wake me in the next room. Once I had been so worried that I ran out in my nightie to hug her while she and Mom stood in the kitchen. She had gently ruffled my hair and said I was a wonderful girl.

Those letters were so lonely and had nowhere to go now. So Mom and I burned them in the sauna stove.

All I put back in the secret compartment was a short beaver-chewed stick - Maggie was always collecting them - wrapped in a strand of pale blue yarn, for the clematis blossoms on Maggie's heart.

And Mom told me something nice. Nels and Mom wanted someone officially named who would take over as my parent in case anything ever happened to them, and they had asked Maggie just before we left for our winter in Labrador. It was sort of symbolic, too — like having a special third parent. She was wild with excitement about it when she agreed. She said it felt like she would have a real family. It was to be a homecoming surprise for me, and there was to be a special sauna to celebrate.

Now it struck me as strange that the person who taught us so much about friendship and trust must have experienced so little of either in her own childhood.

In the glove compartment I found a business card. It was from a tattoo artist who lived on the Vermont side of the Connecticut River. "Specializing in Wildlife, Myth, and Goddess motifs." Then in parentheses, "No Biker Art."

In September I headed east to a small New England college on the coast of Maine. I drove there in Maggie's truck. On the way, I detoured to see the tattoo artist. I felt comfortable with him right off. He was a calm, friendly kind of guy with a graying ponytail who listened carefully to what I wanted. He even had reference material that provided ideas and poses, and he promised to look up more in the Dartmouth College Library, which was just upstream on the New Hampshire side. I provided the sketches I had drawn for ideas and he nodded, even complimented me on the drawings.

"I want to stay within these lines," I said, defining the boundary by tracing my finger along the top of the legs of my jeans. " That's what a modest swimsuit will cover for those times I'll have to swim in a public place."

He showed me portfolios of his extraordinary artwork, then explained the procedures, care, follow-up, and what to expect. He brought out his tools, showed me the autoclave that sterilized them, and demystified everything about the process.

"Since your tattoo involves intimate surfaces, you need to bring a friend," he advised. "That'll make it easier for both of us. Your friend will be a calming presence for you, and will witness that I do nothing untoward while I'm working on your tattoo. I have to protect myself that way. Or I can hire a female nurse to be present, but that will cost more."

"Thanks, I didn't think of that," I said, while suppressing the sudden thought that of course I'd bring Maggie. Sometimes I just forgot she wasn't around. "I'll bring someone."

"I'm a registered nurse in real life. My equipment is state-of-the-art and clean. I guess you already saw that. And one final thing. You'll need to shave the place for the last track."

I felt a little in need of reassurance. "It's not too strange, what I want for the last track?"

"No, it's a great idea. That is your personal wilderness, and as you said, it's important that the tracks hold wilderness," he said understandingly. "Just to give you some comparison, I'll show you the intimate zone portfolio if you wish. You're tame by a long shot. Very conservative."

"I'd like to see it."

Afterwards we scheduled three different two-hour sessions spread over two days. He didn't think he'd need all that time, but wanted to allow for the unexpected. He also gave me a print-out of how to take care of the work for the two weeks afterwards, before allowing exposure to air, sun, or showing the artwork. The $180.00 an hour fee and two weeks of fussy follow-up care made me gulp pretty hard, but I was determined. When we shook hands, he and I knew I'd be back as planned.

As I drove the rest of the way to college, I had plenty to think about. I had to admit that I wasn't as wild as I thought, and that I was shocked at some of the intimate places people had chosen to have tattooed.

Fall trimester at school was truly exciting. I learned that I had been hopelessly happy and sheltered. People teased me about my "Midwest nice" just as much as I was critical of their suspicious urban cynicism and aggressive righteousness. Perhaps we tempered each other, although I suspect my eyes bugged out wider and longer than theirs did, no matter how much my trusting naiveté astonished them.

In one class I was able to return to my awful attempts at illustrating A Tribe Like Us. The library had a translation of the Kalevala that was illustrated with stunning Nordic art that inspired me. I plunged back into the project with new skill and discipline, but the best part was an excellent teacher. Not only was my art teacher skilled with several media, but she also taught Women's Literature and other Women's Studies topics from the point of view of creativity, politics, culture, and psychology. I was thriving, even though I missed my family and friends and couldn't wait for the break that lasted from Thanksgiving to New Year's. It would be plenty long enough for a visit home. There would be so many stories to tell.

The long drive home was made easier by sharing it with another student as far as Sault Saint Marie. We shared gas expenses and slept in the camper behind all-night convenience stores. Only once did a friendly small town cop in Ontario ask us to move on. He was so apologetic and explained that someone had called complaining that a couple of girls were chopping up pallets behind Bud's Easy Stop. We showed him the stove in the camper and our little heap of firewood, and he gave us directions to another place we could park. Then he had us follow him to a small hardwood mill, and the owner gave us a whole bunch of birch and maple ends all cut up small. The cop said he'd drive by in his cruiser to check on us, and he did. We heard him pass by twice.

I called home an hour shy of arriving, to let Nels and Mom know I was almost there. When I pulled into the driveway at the research station, we all collided outside. Mark, Roberta, and Amanda were hardly patient enough for Nels and Mom to greet me first. Smoke was streaming from the sauna chimney, and I guess the sight of that was what let the happy tears out. It had been more than three months since my last sauna and visit with my family. We were all new people now, ready to be reacquainted.

Supper was already cooked and waiting in the oven of the big woodstove in Roberta's kitchen. It would still be warm whenever we were ready. Amanda, not Roberta, had made all the bread, and it smelled heavenly.

"I'd like a few minutes when we enter with just ladies, if that's OK," I requested.

Before we entered the dressing room, Amanda blurted. "Oh, I can't wait to see! Is it like Maggie's or even better?"

"Not better, but it's as good."

On the top slope of each buttock, just below the small of my back, was a beautiful wolverine. Their coloring was perfect, like watercolors over fine detailed ink drawings. Each tail flowed toward the notch between the cheeks, and the wolverines faced away as if they were about to go around the hips. One was pale, like Ghost, and he looked back over his shoulder. He was above the right cheek. The darker one on the left was intent, ready to travel and already mid-stride.

Below each, emerging from the notch, a sinuous line of tracks parted, and gracefully curved under each wolverine and on around each hip in a wavy line. Each track was deft and incredibly detailed and shaded. On the right, the tracks beneath Ghost were subtly faded, growing lighter as they turned the corner. The last track was faint and ethereal, and at the iliac crest they disappeared altogether. On the left the tracks were strong and bold right to the end. I parted the hair that hid the final print.

"This one is for a lover to discover. It's for Maggie and mystery and the sacredness of the wilds. That's how I want to remember what I learned from her."

"It's beautiful, Kristin, although it's nothing I'd do myself," said Roberta. "I didn't expect this, even with you requesting a minute for ladies only."

Amanda was quiet, but looked hard at how Ghost's tracks disappeared.

Mom hadn't said a word. I was terrified that she would disapprove, or want to know how big a chunk of those months of waitressing were tossed away for body art, but when I turned to look, she was lost in the sweetest expression she could have possibly had. Then great big silent tears rolled out of her eyes. She opened the door to the outside.

"Come on, you guys," she called to Mark and Nels. "You need to see the wolverines. They loop around and around the whole world."

When we went to the benches there was great quiet. No one sat where Maggie usually did, but the first sprinkle of water was to her memory. It was one of the first times since her dying that I wasn't sad thinking of her. Something — some sense of her presence — made me feel full and grateful, instead of drained and longing.

Mom and I lingered for another session after the others went up to supper. I am just a bit taller than she is. She's in her mid-forties and, to me, stunningly beautiful. There are wonderful sun, wind, and sky wrinkles around her eyes. Her hands are strong and brown and show the fine creases of outdoor work. The rest of her body is still tight and smooth and muscular. I think she's at the best she'll ever be — gracefully balancing at the edge of middle age. Since I saw her last, the hair at the corners of her forehead has gone to silver — the exact strands that she pulls back to be clasped by a clip or incorporated into a braid. It looks great. I told her so, and she said that Nels likes it too.

We sat back to back on the top bench, leaning on each other with equal pressure, like bookends on a shelf.

"Mari, do you remember telling me the story of the tracks on your leg when I was 10?" I asked, thinking of saunas long ago.

"Tonight I was remembering it with great clarity," she said. "I hadn't recalled it for years, though."

"Who would have thought it would take us all those places? Or bring us here now?"

"Do you have a sweetheart?" she asked, sounding like a good friend more than a concerned mother.

"Not at the moment, but there is someone I like a lot who will be in Winter Ecology with me next term," I admitted. "I'm fussy and cautious. He'll have to measure up. He likes to dance those New England contras and squares like Maggie, and he plays the squeeze-box. Dancing was the only thing she missed out here, wasn't it?"

"I think so." Mom paused a little. "And now I miss her fiddle playing. But something will show up. Something or someone will follow some tracks, or make some tracks, and things will all come around in place. They even have those dances around here now. A band called Duck for the Oyster comes over from Wisconsin now and then, and I've seen posters for dances with Circle of Friends and Wild Thyme. We should go while you're here."

123

"Oh, we have to Mom! I've been learning. It's really easy and they walk you through first. You'll love it."

"Well, let's get cooled off and eat. I'm glad you're home."

When we stood up, Mom put her hands on my shoulders and gave me a long look. It was the look mothers give children thousands of times in their lives – direct and deep, full of wonder and pride and spiced with a dash of fear, a plea for caution and goodness. I felt lucky that we were such good friends, that the distinctions of age difference, of child and parent, had faded.

An owl calls as two women emerge from the sauna. They walk close enough that their shoulders bump and touch lightly until they reach a truck with a wooden camper. Their fingertips trail oh so lightly along it as they walk by. They embrace briefly. Their voices drift among dark trees and across the lake before they enter a door to find supper.

"You ever wonder where Kwewadzsho is?"
"All the time. But she's never far away, really."

Garrett Conover

Garrett Conover has been drawn to strong independent people and the wildest places for as long as he can remember. He was born in the Berkshire Hills of Massachusetts in 1955 to adventurous parents who loved camping, climbing, and skiing. Parental influences started early from a liberal naturalist mother and an engineer father who, when not at work, was a folk singing, artistic guy with a wacky sense of humor.

Garrett seems to have perfected the art of making do in rural places, or at least has been remarkably lucky. School and college took him to Vermont Academy, the University of Montana, and College of the Atlantic in Maine. Adjacent wilds seemed to be the primary focus, and snowshoes, skis, and a fly rod the tools of inquiry. The last recorded attempt at promoting Garrett's scholarly excellence left a high school guidance counselor clutching his exasperated head. He had earnestly asked, "Have you considered the academic credentials of your college choices?" Sensing this was a leading question, Garrett was too shy to admit that he hadn't, and too naïve to refrain from pointing out on a map that University of Montana was only a few hours from three federal Wilderness Areas.

Since 1980, Garrett and his wife Alexandra have been leading wilderness trips through their guiding service North Woods Ways. Each year finds them canoeing in the open water seasons and snowshoeing with toboggans in the winter. The trips are primarily in Northern Maine, with annual visits to Labrador or Quebec for longer trips. Occasionally they have led winter trips in the Boundary Waters Canoe Area Wilderness of Minnesota.

Garrett is the author of Beyond the Paddle, and co-author with Alexandra of The Snow Walker's Companion. Kristin's Wilderness is his first foray into fiction.

Garrett and Alexandra make their home in a permanent wall tent next to a beautiful log sauna along the Big Wilson Stream in central Maine. A short walk through the woods brings them to their road-edge office and outfitting building.

Rod MacIver

Erase the lines: I pray you not to love classifications.
The thing is like a river, from source to sea-mouth
One flowing life.

- Robinson Jeffers, Monument

Rod MacIver has been a self-employed artist since 1995. He offers both originals and limited edition prints through his website, Heron Dance. Rod makes his images available to grassroots wilderness protection groups for use without charge.

"Since about the age of eight, my life and art has been nourished and inspired by time in wild places, by cycles larger than the concerns of humans. The deep silence and deep peace, and yes even the great struggle to cling to life, the precious gift of life, are at the center of my work. I try to express reverence for the mystery and beauty of wild places. I try to honor the places I love and the sense of freedom I've found there.

"The delicacy and flow of watercolor constantly urges me to simplify, to minimize, to express the spirit and essence rather than the detail. I try and try and fail and try again with the hope that over time the spirit of what Robinson Jeffers refers to as "the river...one flowing life" might gradually emerge."

Rod MacIver is founder of Heron Dance, a non-profit organization that publishes the magazine Heron Dance Journal, as well as many books, blank journals, and cards with Rod's art. You can find out more at www.herondance.org or by requesting a catalog at 888-304-3766.

Tanya Thompson

Tanya's art brings her vibrancy and fluidity as she feels connected to all living things, including the people who enjoy her work. Art and yoga are both important aspects of her spiritual practice. She makes her home in Ely, MN on the edge of a beautiful wilderness. She can be contacted at ravengirlinely@yahoo.com